MW01701073

Murders

Suddenly, a muffled sound from Dan's office caught her by surprise. There was second sound. She turned the knob and opened the door. "Dan! I'm glad you're back, because ..." Dan Fisher lay sprawled on the floor in front of his desk. Crimson blood covered his head. Katie stopped and stared down at him, then kneeled beside him. "Dan? Oh Dan!" she screamed out in horror. The door at the back of the office opened slightly and a small, black, handgun pointed out at her. She screamed in horror and ran, slamming the door behind her as a bullet smashed the door frame. She raced down the hall for the open elevator doors at the opposite end. "Wait! Don't go!"

The Dark Hill Murders

by

Robert Ziegler

Commonwealth
Publications

If you purchased this book without a cover, you should be aware that this book is stolen property. It was reported as "unsold and destroyed" to the publisher, and neither the author nor the publisher has received any payment for this "stripped book."

A Commonwealth Publications Paperback
THE DARK HILL MURDERS

This edition published 1996
by Commonwealth Publications
9764 - 45th Avenue,
Edmonton, AB, CANADA T6E 5C5
All rights reserved
Copyright © 1994 by Robert Ziegler

ISBN: 1-896329-78-0

No part of this book may be reproduced or utilized in any form or by any means, electronic or mechanical, including photocopying, recording, or by any information storage and retrieval system, without permission in writing from the publisher.

This work is a novel and any similarity to actual persons or events is purely coincidental.

Printed in Canada
Designed by: Danielle Monlezun
Cover Illustration by: Pat Bidwell

Chapter One

Two minutes to five. Am I ever glad this day's over! In her worst nightmare, Katie Denton couldn't possibly have imagined the deadly, horrid events of the next few minutes as she glanced up at the wall clock. She got up from behind her sleek, white, metal receptionist's desk, turned off the IBM Computer and walked over to the huge window. She loved her spectacular view from the tenth floor of the Market Street Bay Building in downtown San Francisco. She looked down at the heavy traffic below momentarily, then returned to her desk and pushed the intercom mode on the telephone. "Dan? I'm leaving. I'll see you tomorrow."

A few silent moments passed. Still no answer. She walked over and knocked lightly on the door to Dan Fisher's inner office. With no answer forthcoming, she grabbed the doorknob. Locked! *What the hell... that's odd. Why'd he lock the door?* She raised the phone to her ear and pressed the record button on the intercom system. "Dan? I'm leaving. Our bet's still on! The Giants'll take the A's tonight in the series. See you tomorrow to collect my winnings."

Katie hung her purse over her shoulder and crossed the plush furnished reception area of Fisher Investment Consultant Inc. Opening the door into the hallway of the tenth floor, she turned the lock on the inner doorknob, closed it and entered the women's restroom directly across the hall. She purposefully placed her black leather purse on the counter and opened it. Her tight, pink skirt and blouse clung sensually on her petite, twenty-three year old frame. Her permed red hair flowed over her shoulders as she brushed it under and over, thoroughly, for a few seconds. Then her lipstick and a final touch of mascara. Her Irish green eyes twinkled in the anticipation of watching the World Series with Bobby and their friends at his condo. *Yes, perfect. This'll keep his eyes on me and only me.* She returned the make-up to her purse, then remembered the second most important package for her man. *His new baseball cap... Battle for the Bay. It's in my desk. Gotta go back and get it.*

Katie hurried across the hall, put her key in the door and opened the office. Darkness filled the room but she didn't recall turning off the lights. She switched them on and opened the bottom desk drawer, quickly lifting out the plastic bag. She glanced up at the clock. *Almost five after five. I'd better get going.* Suddenly, a muffled sound from Dan's office caught her by surprise. There was second sound. She turned the knob and opened the door. "Dan! I'm glad you're back, because ..." Dan Fisher lay sprawled on the floor in front of his desk. Crimson blood covered his head. Katie stopped and stared down at him, then kneeled beside him. "Dan? Oh Dan!" she screamed out in horror. The door at the back of the office opened slightly and a small, black, handgun pointed out at her. She screamed in horror and ran, slamming the door behind her as a bullet smashed the door frame. She raced down the hall for the open elevator doors at the opposite end. "Wait! Don't go!" Her hysterical scream reverberated through the tenth floor.

Suddenly, the floor began to shake, gently at first. "Oh shit, oh God! Help!" The building rumbled and swayed as she glanced back over her shoulder for a sign of the person in her office. Someone exited. Then the lights flickered out, engulfing the hall in pitch blackness. A loud rumbling echoed through the hall and the floor shook violently beneath her feet.

Screams of terror filled the hall of the tenth floor from behind office doors. Katie fell onto the carpeted floor in front of the open elevator. Security lights at each end of the hall flashed on, illuminating the constantly shaking and swaying hallway in an eerie glow as the earth quaked violently under the building.

Suddenly, a pair of strong hands picked Katie up from the floor and twisted her arms tightly behind her back. She felt a violent shove. Her body crashed against the wall beside the elevator opening and fell to the floor. Her arms absorbed the brunt of the sharp, searing pain when she hit the moving floor in front of the dark opening of the elevator shaft. The elevator had gone.

"No! Don't! Help!" she screamed. Terrified, Katie struggled against the movement of the floor, trying to regain her feet. Suddenly, the strong hands pushed her sharply from behind, thrusting her forward into the black abyss of the open elevator shaft. Her fall abruptly ended when she crashed into the top of the elevator, half a floor below. Katie, knocked unconscious when her head bounced off the steel supports on the roof of the elevator, was mercifully saved from the pain.

Frantic screams for help filled the hallway. People ran out of the many offices in the Bay Building in an effort to escape the swaying building as San Francisco shook violently from a massive earthquake. The murderer disappeared with the crowd into the east stairway and descended to safety, leaving Katie Denton lying unconscious on top of the elevator, and Dan Fisher dead on the floor of his office.

Chapter Two

Moments before the quake hit, Brandon Harrison raised his binoculars to his gleaming brown eyes across town at Candlestick Park. They were the same black Leupolds that he had used on hundreds of investigative stakeouts during his career as a private investigator. From his second level seat between first base and right field, he stared excitedly at Will Clark, the Giants' first baseman and top slugger. Harrison felt incredibly fortunate to have had those seats given to him by an old friend; especially fortunate because it was the World Series.

1989 had seen the Giants and the Oakland A's battle out the first two games in Oakland, across the bay. The A's had taken them both. Now they were on the Giants' home turf, Candlestick Park, and the third game was almost ready to start.

"Hey, Brandon! Here... take these hot dogs!" He turned around in his seat to see Tina Wolffe, his girlfriend and partner in the agency, step carefully down the stadium stairs two rows behind him. She carried a cardboard tray on which four large hot dogs, two light beers and an order of nachos were precariously balanced. The handsome, well-built, tanned, six-foot P.I. stood and plucked off the two paper cups of beer from the tray, lightening her load.

"Thanks. I almost lost 'em." Like Brandon, Tina wore an official Giants cap clipped onto her straight black hair which was curled slightly under, above her shoulders. Dark green, black-trimmed sunglasses hid her excited, sparkling brown, Eurasian eyes. Faded blue jeans and a white Giants sweatshirt clung tightly to her youthful, petite, nicely curved figure. At twenty-five, this was her first World Series.

"This place is packed! There must be a hundred thousand people here."

"You're probably right." She carefully walked in four seats to their reserved seating and gingerly sat down. Brandon sat beside her. "Take your hot dogs, and here's napkins."

"Got 'em." He smiled and kissed her cheek,and handed her a beer. "Thanks for going for food and drinks."

"Anything for you, my love." They each sipped on their beer and gazed happily into each other's eyes. "When does the game start?"

"Let's see... it's almost five after five. It'll start in about... God damn!" Suddenly, the stadium rumbled and violently shook beneath their seats. What had sounded like a cheer from the capacity filled stadium, turned into a combined gasp of terror. The concrete stadium rippled up and down with the continuous earth movement, violently knocking pieces of the stadium onto the crowd. The stadium lights flickered twice and then it went dark.

Tina and Brandon jumped up simultaneously, ready to flee for safer ground. "Earthquake! Brandon!" Tina screamed, spilling her nachos over the concrete floor as the four hot dogs fell to their feet. She ripped off her sunglasses and stared in bewilderment at the overhead stadium light towers swaying ominously above the capacity filled stadium. The full force of the massive earthquake violently shook Candlestick Park up, down, back and forth for nearly fifteen seconds.

Then it was over. Several people sat back down, while others began to make their way into the crowd, toward the exits. Then the murmuring and excited voices of over sixty thousand people asking each other what happened, filled the air. "Shit! That was a monster! I wonder how big it was? I wonder if they'll still play," were the continual, recurring themes of conversation as the baseball fans began the desperate evacuation into the darkened stadium aisles of Candlestick and out to the vast parking lot for safety.

"Oh God, that was a big one!"

"The Big One?"

Tina watched the crowd in horrified silence, wondering what they should do. She felt Brandon's arm wrapped securely around her waist. Her body began to tremble with fear as she watched the thousands of people hasten, in a seemingly unreal, orderly fashion. Guided by the park employees and security people with flashlights waving in the near darkness of the stadium, the exodus was orderly and relatively calm. A police car drove out onto the playing field and announced, "Ladies and Gentlemen. Those in the upper level are being asked to evacuate the premises immediately."

Brandon took a sip of his beer. "Damn, it could've been 'The Big One'." They stared at each other. "What'd you think? Should we try to get out of here?"

"It looks like that's what everyone else has in mind."

"Yeah. Let's sit down and wait. I don't wanna get caught in a crowd if there's an aftershock."

They sat down uneasily as the crowd fled past. Tina looked down at the spilled nachos and cheese on the floor. "My nachos!"

"Well, at least we didn't unwrap the Candle Sticks." He reached down, retrieved all four wrapped hot dogs, sat up and winked at her. "And, we didn't even spill a drop of beer."

"Shit, Brandon! How can you take this so

lightly? That was one hell of an earthquake. There could be people who are hurt, or dead out there."

"You're right. I'm just scared I guess."

"Yeah." Tina gazed into his concerned eyes, then reached down and picked up the hot dogs. "Let's eat these. I get hungry when I'm nervous like this... not being able to do anything."

"I know. Sure, let's eat. We've got to keep our strength up, just in case."

"I hate earthquakes," she whispered.

Just then, an announcement from the police bull horn echoed throughout the stadium. "The third game of the world series is being postponed. Everyone is being asked to evacuate the stadium." Lines of thousands of people, in a mass exodus from the stadium, streamed past them. The players on both teams left the playing field. Crowds of fans poured out of the concrete building onto the open grassy field, seeking refuge and safety in the event of another quake.

When the initial throng of people had finally departed, leaving the seats vacated around them, Brandon decided it was time to find out just how much damage the quake had caused. Their hot dogs eaten and their beer drained to the last drop, the two private investigators left their seats and hurried through the nearly empty Candlestick Stadium, out to the parking lot.

A news van, parked just outside the main exit of the stadium, was surrounded by a huge crowd of onlookers, anxious to be interviewed about their experiences during the quake. A monitor inside the van was visible to the crowd. The reports of damage were just beginning to come in from all around the bay area. Scenes of the collapsed portion of the Oakland Bay Bridge shocked the onlookers. Videos of the fires around the city served to emphasize the seriousness of the earthquake, and rumors that San Francisco had just experienced the 'Big One' circulated through the crowd.

Brandon and Tina looked on in astounded curiosity as the mobile news broadcaster commented on the events and scenes as they became known to him. Tina stared at the scene of the westbound Bay Bridge, a five lane upper span, which collapsed upon the lower eastbound span. She flinched in horror when she recognized the Interstate 880 Cypress Freeway in West Oakland, leading to the Bay Bridge, collapse upon itself. The catastrophe was real.

"Brandon?" An aftershock rolled under their feet for several seconds. She threw her arms around his shoulders and stared up at the stadium, hoping that it wouldn't collapse on them.

"It's okay. Just a strong aftershock."

"Can we go home?"

"I don't know, but we should try."

"We don't have to cross any bridges, do we?"

"Several." He looked into her uncertain eyes, knowing exactly what she meant.

Chapter Three

A dense, gray fog had rolled in from the Pacific, across San Francisco Bay in the early morning hours. It blanketed the Golden Gate Bridge, engulfing it and the city, as if to hide the extreme damage caused by Mother Nature's destructive outburst two days earlier.

Brandon Harrison sleepily gazed out of his large dining room window and sipped on a second cup of coffee, contemplating the fog and the many aftershocks. From his view high above the city, in his beautiful Mount Sutro home, Brandon saw the tops of the Golden Gate peaking through the upper layer of the fog bank in the distance. He knew that the gloomy gray fog would dissipate by ten or so, leaving a drizzling rain and giving way to another cool October day in The City by the Bay.

There had been no power or water in the two days following the 7.1 quake. Most people had to obtain their food and water by waiting in long lines outside the few convenience stores that remained open, or at local government shelters.

Tina sat opposite him, across the table. Dressed in purple warm-up sweats, her shoulder length black hair was pulled back and pinned up on top of her head, in preparation for her morning jog.

A loud knock echoed through their home, startling the two private investigators. Brandon looked up at her. "It's eight a.m. We expecting anybody?"

"No! I'll go see." She put her coffee cup down, then strolled quickly across the living room and opened the front door.

"Help me!" Tina, confronted by an hysterical young woman, flinched momentarily. "You are a private investigator!"

"Yes... this is Harrison-Wolffe Investigations." The woman stared nervously at Tina, then turned and eyed the quiet neighborhood street behind her. Her dark red hair was permed and brushed back in waves, held in place with thick hairspray. Red freckles spotted her cute, youthful, mid-twenties face and large, secretary glasses covered her worried green eyes and small pug nose. She appeared to be exhausted, showing signs of a lack of sleep with dark circles under her eyes. She wore tight-fitting, faded blue Levi's jeans, and a red U.C. Berkeley sweatshirt and white Nike athletic shoes.

Tina put out her hand in a friendly gesture. The red headed woman looked behind her, to the street, then pushed past Tina, slamming the door. "Please lock it." Tina turned the dead bolt.

"Come with me into the next room," Tina said, curious. Katie Denton smiled nervously, then followed her into the dining room, where Brandon sat at the table reading the newspaper on the events of October 17th and 18th.

"Brandon Harrison, this is, I'm sorry, I didn't catch your name."

"Katie Denton." Harrison stood up, smiled warmly and shook her hand in a delicate greeting. He motioned the woman to have a seat across from him at the highly polished, dark maple table.

"Would you like coffee?"

"Thank you." She sat opposite him. Tina poured a mug of freshly brewed coffee from the small percolator on a Coleman gas camp stove, located on the adjacent kitchen counter. She placed the hot cup in front of the nervous woman, pulled out a chair beside Brandon, and sat down.

Katie poured a little milk into her coffee and stirred it, keeping her eyes averted from theirs for several seconds of strained silence.

"Well... Miss Denton. Perhaps you'd like to tell us what this is all about?" Brandon leaned forward, his voice cautious.

Finally, Katie looked up into his dark brown, questioning eyes. The defiant look on her tired face seemed to fade as their eyes met for a moment. Her arms reached out, her white delicate fingers beckoning him to listen, to help. Katie's voice cried out painfully. "I don't know where to start. It's so awful."

"How about from the beginning?"

"Someone murdered my boss."

Brandon nearly choked on a sip of hot coffee, then leaned forward, his curiosity piqued. "Murder? Did you see this murder take place?"

"Yes... no... but..." Tears filled her tired eyes.

"That's okay. Tell me what you saw." Brandon's mannerisms were calm and professional, easing her anxious feelings.

"Will you help me? I don't know how long I can go on like this. I think he's gonna kill me too!" Tears of fear began rolling from her darkened, tired eyes.

"This sounds like a matter for the police."

"The police? Shit! A killer's stalking me and they can't spare anyone because of the earthquake."

"Okay, Miss Denton. Start from the beginning. Tell me exactly what happened." They stared at each other momentarily, then she took a deep breath and began as Brandon stood up to refill his cup.

"I'm, was, a legal secretary for Fisher Investments, in the Bay Building. It was Tuesday, just before the quake hit. I left a message for Dan Fisher that I was leaving."

"You were leaving?" asked Tina.

"Yes, it was five o'clock. See, he was in his office, the door locked. It was weird, because he never locks his office door. And I don't know who was inside with him or if he was even there. I just left a message for him on his office answering machine saying that I was going home."

"I see. So you don't know if he was in his office or not." Brandon placed his hands on the back of the highly polished mahogany chair and leaned forward, looking into her tearful green eyes. Tina sat beside her and jotted down notes on the conversation.

"That's right."

"Go on."

"Well, I went into the rest room to kinda freshen up before going to some friends' house to watch the game. I remembered that I'd forgot something in my desk, so I returned to the office to get it."

"How long were you in the rest room do you think?"

"Oh, maybe five minutes at the most. I'm really not sure." Katie looked down at her hands and twisted a gold diamond ring slowly around her right ring finger, her mind carefully contemplating the events as she remembered them. "Anyway, I went back into the office and opened the bottom drawer and got my package. Then I heard it!"

"What was that?"

"Well, it sounded like... something dropping on the floor. I wasn't sure what it was, but it came from Dan's office. It was a kinda thump sound. I turned the doorknob, and it was unlocked. I opened it. Dan was laying on the floor, covered in blood."

She winced as if in pain and stared up at Brandon. Her eyes became moist with tears as the painful vision replayed itself for possibly the hundredth time in her mind. "I touched him, but he was dead!" Her voice cried out in horror, tears pouring from her eyes. She collapsed face down into her crossed arms on the table top.

Tina moved quickly to the anguished woman's side. "How do you know he was dead?"

"He was... the blood... I just knew it."

Brandon walked slowly around the table past her, then sat down in the chair that Tina had occupied, facing Katie. His voice was gentle but firm, as he continued questioning, in an effort to keep the tired and anguished woman's story unfolding to them. "Did you see the murderer?"

"Yes... kind of. See... he had a gun in his hand. He was behind the door. He had a gun!"

"You saw him, then."

"No, I had to get away. It all happened so fast. I slammed the door and ran out into the hallway. That's when the earthquake hit."

"Did he chase you?"

"Yes, but the building began to move and shake, and I lost my balance. Then the lights went out! I tried to make it to the open elevator, but I fell! I was terrified! The elevator was dark and the doors were still open."

Katie's eyes painfully widened as if searching for a way to escape the nightmare, that terrible memory, for the next few moments. "Then I felt those hands pick me up off of the floor. He threw me into the elevator, but it wasn't there! All I remember is a feeling of terror. Then I woke up in the hospital."

A few moments of uneasy silence fell over them, while Brandon analyzed her story. He looked down at the newspaper on the table and opened it to the third page. His eyes scanned the column to the lower right hand side.

Woman Rescued On Elevator. Her name was printed plainly in the story of how rescue workers had found her on the roof of an elevator which had been stuck between the ninth and tenth floors in the Bay Building. Building security discovered her while climbing down into the shaft, trying to free several trapped people inside the elevator.

Then, his eyes caught the small article on the adjoining page:

Murder on Market Street. The Fisher Investment Office, in the Bay Building on Market Street, was the scene of the grisly murder of its owner, Dan Fisher. The discovery was made late yesterday during a search of the building.

Brandon's eyes looked up from the paper. Tina stared at him, an inquisitive but knowing expression on her face. She knew by the look on his face that he'd found a piece of corroborating evidence to confirm her story.

"We may have problems if the killer read the paper." Tina walked over to him and followed his finger pointing at the two stories. She began to silently read as Katie looked across the table into Brandon's eyes.

"What?"

"Your name's in this article, and how you were rescued. If the murderer read it, he knows who you are, and that you're alive!"

"Brandon? Did you read this one on Dan Fisher's murder?"

"Yeah, earlier this morning."

"There's one on Dan? Let me see." Katie quickly made her way around the table and began to read the article with Tina.

"Detective Garth made a statement about the murder. He's probably in charge of the investigation."

Katie Denton stared at the paper, silently assimilating the information. "See? Dan's dead! Now do you believe me?" She sobbed. "I need to use your bathroom."

"Of course. It's right down this hall past the kitchen, on the right." Tina got up and led the way, pointing at the bathroom door at the end of the short hall which led to the den.

Their guest entered the bathroom and the two detectives met at the sliding glass door to the outside deck, exiting for a quick conference. Brandon's eyes followed Market Street far below them at the bottom of the hill, across to the Bay Bridge. The fog had almost completely dissipated and the bridge stood empty in the morning light. He couldn't see the damaged portion of the huge double deck structure, but he knew that the bridge and the entire city would require considerable amount of time to repair, both physically and psychologically.

"She's devastated, just like the city." Tina leaned against the redwood railing on the deck and gazed out at the city. "The fires are out and people are digging out, trying to regain some semblance of their lives before the quake."

"Yes. And Miss Denton, is she on the level? What'd you think?"

Suddenly, a loud gun blast ripped through the bathroom window, then another. Tina jumped, then stared into Brandon's astonished eyes. "What the hell...?"

Katie's horrified scream pierced the house. She threw open the door and ran frantically down the hall toward them, her frightened eyes stared back as if pursued by a demon.

Brandon jumped through the opening, followed by Tina close on his heels. He grabbed his nine millimeter Beretta from the kitchen counter, then sprinted across the living room and out the front door. Taking cover behind the green, bush-covered railing, he saw the red late model Ford pickup truck turn left down the block, its wheels screeching loudly on the pavement. He leveled his gun at the truck, but couldn't get off a shot before it left his field of vision.

Brandon turned to see the front bathroom window shattered. Several neighbors had stepped outside their homes to see what the commotion was all about. He slipped the weapon under his belt, knowing what they must be thinking of him. He ignored them.

Damn! Someone's either taking target practice on my house or... she's in serious trouble.

Chapter Four

Detective Harry Garth, of the San Francisco Police Department, held tight to his desk at police headquarters and frowned. His intense, tired blue eyes closed as he rode out the long, rumbling aftershock. The mild quake felt like it was probably a 4.6. He was starting to get used to the feeling of the building moving under him. It didn't matter where he'd been in the past two days, but whenever one of the dozens of aftershocks had hit, Garth had been above the ground, inside a swaying building.

The loud, rumbling noise that accompanied the shaker faded, and his desk stopped rattling. Harry opened his eyes to see that his coffee mug had spilled its freshly brewed contents onto some paperwork. The rest of the officers, detectives, volunteers and assorted people within the huge, desk- filled room, breathed a collective sigh of relief, and the constant murmur of excited voices once again filled the room that had been quieted during the aftershock.

Power had been restored to most of the city during the last couple of hours, making Harry's job a little easier. It had been less than forty hours since the massive October 17th earthquake came rumbling out of its epicenter, 60 miles south of San Francisco, near Los Gatos, peaking on the Richter scale at 7.1. The resulting horror of its devastation was just settling in on the entire Bay area.

He got up slowly from his desk and walked over to a large window. From his location on the second floor of City Hall, he looked down at Van Ness Avenue, west past Russian Hill, toward the Pacific. The fires were out now, and rescue teams were digging through collapsed buildings in a desperate search for survivors still buried under tons of debris.

After a long night of unrestful sleep, sleep caused by three major aftershocks, he was back on the job and ready to help wherever the captain assigned his team. Usually, Detective Harry Garth would be investigating one of the many homicides that had taken place during the night, but last night had been quiet. Time was of the essence, the department had to concentrate all of its resources on finding survivors of the killer quake.

He sipped on his cup of lukewarm coffee and read over his assignment for the morning. *The Marina District again. Divisadero and Lomard streets, to coordinate a search of severely damaged and collapsed apartment buildings.* He frowned at the thought of what he might find under these ruins, and put on his light brown, tweed sports coat, then turned to meet the familiar face of an old friend across the room.

"Hey, Harry! Look who's here to see you!" His partner of six years, Detective Phil Black, stood in the doorway which led out to the elevators and the main hall. He grinned, then looked back into the hall and motioned to someone to enter. Garth watched curiously as he stuffed his assignment papers into a side coat pocket. Phil had put on a brown trench coat to hide his rumpled gray suit. His hair, thick dark brown and relatively long, with ear-length sideburns, was combed straight back in a style that reminded him of Elvis. He could tell that Phil hadn't had much sleep last night by the tired look in his usually gleaming, alert blue eyes.

Garth stretched his lean, six foot body and impatiently awaited the appearance of his partner's unexpected visitor, then, unconsciously, ran his fingers through his light blond, thinning hair.

He and Phil had gone through the Academy together over fifteen years ago, and served as uniformed officers for nine years in separate areas of the city. The two men were finally brought together as partners in the homicide division. They were both going to celebrate their big fortieth next July, a somewhat unsettling feeling to him.

Harry then saw the unexpected but welcome visitor walk through the door. "Harrison," he muttered to himself, then smiled and walked through the crowded office toward him. They met midway through the room at Black's desk and greeted each other with reserved but friendly acknowledgment. "Harrison, what brings you out in earthquake weather?"

"Harry! You're looking a bit tired. Been putting in some long hours on overtime these past two days?" Brandon sat on the edge of the desk, Harry on the edge of an adjoining desk and Phil Black stood between them, arms crossed.

"Yeah. It's bad out there. Amazingly enough, we haven't really had the death count I expected after our original survey of the damage."

"I hear most of the deaths are being attributed to the collapse of the Nimitz. They're estimating two hundred and fifty-three, died there."

Harry frowned momentarily, recalling the totals on the morning news talk show which he listened to every day on his way in to work. "The death toll's climbed to two hundred and seventy-four now, and the rescue workers haven't even really begun to dig into rubble of the Nimitz and the marina area here."

"Not to mention the damage further south, toward the epicenter in Los Gatos," Phil Black interjected, recalling his search for information on damage in the Palo Alto area, where his family was located. Phil sat down in his desk chair, rolled backward a little, then picked up his lukewarm coffee cup and took a long sip.

"I'm interested in one particular death, one not related to the earthquake." Brandon stared into Harry Garth's eyes and smiled confidently.

"Yeah? Which one?"

"Dan Fisher, Market Street. I understand that you're working on the case."

"Was, Brandon," He paced a few steps in front of him, turned and leaned against the desk again. "It's been put on hold during the cleanup. What's your interest in the Fisher case?"

"I've got a client who asked me to investigate."

"Yeah? Well, I haven't got much on it, and probably won't for a while. If you're gonna look into the case, keep me informed."

"I'll try. So, what've you got?"

"Fisher was found on the floor of his office Tuesday night, with a bullet in his head. His secretary was found later, during a rescue of people stuck in the elevator, between the ninth and tenth floors of the same building, the Bay Building. She says that the man who killed Fisher tried to kill her by pushing her into the elevator shaft!"

"Any ballistics on the slug yet?"

"Yeah, but I haven't had time to go over the report yet!"

"See if you can match it up to these," He handed two slugs to the surprised Garth. "I dug 'em outta my bathroom wall."

"Twenty-two caliber, I'd say. What's this gotta do with the Fisher Case?"

"These bullets were meant for his legal secretary, Katie Denton."

Harry frowned. Black picked up a report from his desk. "The ballistics report," He handed it to Garth, who quickly scanned it for vital information that would reveal the weapon used on the victim. "Looks like a small thirty-two caliber, not a twenty-two." He handed the report to Brandon.

Brandon read over the information to satisfy his own curiosity, then handed it back to Phil Black. "A small thirty-two; one would've had to get pretty close to Fisher to put a hole in his head like that." Harry nodded and stood up to leave.

"Or, an awfully good shot. Come on, Phil. We've gotta get down to the Marina."

Phil stood up and followed his partner and Harrison back through the overcrowded police headquarters, through the double doors, and into the busy corridor. They walked past the elevator and descended down the main stairway into the lobby. It too, was overcrowded. There was a large crowd of anxious, agitated victims of the quake, who had recently been evacuated from their homes and were awaiting assistance in locating adequate housing and relief.

They were middle class, displaced families; victims of the killer quake. Angry and disquieted, questioning faces met Harrison's eyes as he moved slowly through the crowds, out the huge plate glass doors and down the steps to Van Ness Avenue.

"Good luck with your investigation, Harrison. Keep in touch."

"You're not gonna mind if I take a look around Fisher's office?"

Brandon's statement stopped Garth in his tracks. He turned in contemplative silence, then stared into Brandon's mischievous brown eyes with a curious, questioning look on his face, "Officially, I can't sanction you to go up there and investigate the murder. The building's open for business again. It didn't sustain any real damage from the quake."

"Thanks, Harry."

"Wait a minute, Harrison! If you find any clues at all, or a shred of evidence, I want you to inform me right away." He furled his eyebrows, a hardened look of determination covering his face. Black stood beside him, the same tough, rugged frown on his face.

The PI turned and quickly descended the front, concrete stairs to the street. He waved, but did not look back at the two police detectives.

"Harrison?"

"You got it!" He grinned, knowing that he'd not really fooled his old friend. It was all a show, a game put on for any observers, such as Garth's partner, Phil Black. He climbed into his silver Porsche 944 parked at the curb in a red no parking zone. He started it up and roared away up an empty Van Ness Avenue.

Five minutes later, after maneuvering around several closed streets, Harrison pulled up in front of the fifteen story, high-rise Bay Building. The massive, new generation, glass-plated structure reflected the morning sun, which burned through the nearly dissipated overcast fog. It resembled a gigantic mirror, reflecting San Francisco's painful resolve to update their buildings in defense of 'The Big One' that broadcasters on every radio station lamented would soon strike, and topple this beautiful city.

Brandon parked across the street from his objective, in a BART station parking lot. Cleanup crews and inspectors were almost the only visible signs of life in the normally bustling, business district. He crossed the street, entered the building, and crossed the lobby to one of four waiting elevators. Alone, he rode in eerie silence up the seismically isolated structure, to the tenth floor.

The hallway was empty, devoid of anyone. He knew that there were probably many people at work, behind closed office doors, replacing fallen pictures from interior walls, re-shelving books and preparing to reopen, in hopes of a return to normal operations. He walked silently on the thick padded carpet, to the Fisher Investments Inc. The door was locked, a yellow police investigation ribbon crisscrossed the entrance.

With a quick wiggle of his favorite lock pick and a twist of the wrist, he opened the door. He smiled wryly to himself, ducked under the ribboned entry, and casually strolled into the expensively furnished reception room. Katie Denton's desk, located at the far end of the large reception room, was still cluttered with debris. A broken, glass-framed picture, which had apparently hit the top of her computer monitor, lay shattered across the desk.

Three wall-sized bookshelves had been totally emptied onto the floor around the room, and the wall clock which had occupied a place opposite the desk, lay unbroken, still keeping the correct time on a contemporary, light beige, pillowed sofa. A matching love seat along the opposite wall held a large, framed painting upside down on its soft pillows. The silk plants that hung from the ceiling in the corners of the reception room, were untouched by the continuous aftershocks of the past two days.

He stepped through the open doorway into the inner office. An outline of where Dan Fisher's body had fallen greeted him, giving him a foreboding sense of danger. His first thoughts after studying the outline of the victim gave Harrison the impression that Fisher had been standing in front of the expensive, large walnut, executive-style desk when he was shot in the forehead. *The killer had to have shot him at fairly close range,* he surmised. *This room's not big enough to have been too far away. A thirty-two caliber... hmm. Looks like the police've gone over the room pretty thoroughly. I wonder...*

He began his search for a clue, a shred of evidence, something that might reveal a motive and a name or two on which to launch the investigation. The desk sat on a forty five degree angle, in front of two, floor-to-ceiling dark oak bookcases, the contents of which had been strewn across the office by the violent force of the massive quake. It appeared that the books had completely covered the body of Dan Fisher after the initial shock.

A doorway led out of the office along the empty shelves in the middle on the back wall. Harrison stepped carefully over the outlined body area and the cluttered hill of books which covered the area in front of the thick, oak door. It was locked with a dead bolt. He turned the lock and opened it. *An executive entrance! I'm not surprised.*

A short passageway led out past a large, private rest room, into the hallway around the corner from the tenth floor's main corridor, where the front door to the office was located. He opened the door, made sure it wasn't locked before closing it, and then purposely made his way along the hall to the door. Cautiously he opened it, peering down toward the front office entrance and the elevators. Harrison noted the proximity of the women's rest room that Katie Denton had used while the killer had entered her employer's office.

The PI contemplated, momentarily, the possible scenarios in which the murderer might have entered the inner office. *He may've waited for Katie to leave, then entered from the executive rest room or maybe they both came in together after she'd gone, unaware that she was across the hall. Fisher probably knew his murderer, to let him get that close.*

He turned and opened the executive entrance numbered 1041-Private, then walked into the rest room. It was not as magnificent and large as Harrison had imagined. He switched on the lights, illuminating the ten by fourteen foot rest room. A large double-sink counter, covered with cream colored three inch tiles, spanned six feet under the counter to the ceiling mirror before him. To the rear was the enclosed toilet.

Brandon walked slowly around the rest room. His prying eyes carefully examined the room, its floor and finally the sink and mirror area. There was no doubt in his mind that the police had gone over every inch of that room, but in the frenzy of multiple aftershocks that swayed the tenth floor, they may have overlooked a crucial piece of evidence, or they may have postponed the thorough investigation until after the rescue of the hundreds of quake victims around the city. He didn't really know, but pursued his investigation anyway.

Methodically, he probed the sink area with a practiced eye. Armed with small tweezers and three, small zip lock baggies, he picked up several small hair strands from the tiled sink. There were two or three dark brown lengths of hair, and many shorter, blond lengths on the counter and in the dry, porcelain sink. Satisfied that he'd located the only two types of hair in the room, Harrison pocketed the baggies, turned off the lights and exited.

Then he noticed it. The door into Fisher's office was closed. *Did I close it?* He reached out and grasped the doorknob. Damn... locked! His inner voice instantly warned him something was amiss. He reached into his pocket, pulled out the lock pick and began to manipulate the keyhole. With a snap and a click, the door unlocked. Cautiously, he pushed the door open slightly, and peered inside. Reaching under his brown, plaid sports coat, he quickly drew his black nine millimeter, semiautomatic Beretta from its holster and slipped a clip into its handle.

Suddenly, the door at the opposite end of the hall burst open. The figure of a man dressed in a black suit, his face unrecognizable through the nylon stocking mask, aimed a small, black, automatic handgun at him and fired twice. Harrison reacted instinctively. He thrust his body through the office door, crashed over the outline of Fisher's body, then dove for cover behind the oak desk. Gun in hand, the PI aimed at the wide open door.

Tense moments passed. He waited behind the desk, his heart pounding fast with the expectation of the assault to come. When it didn't, Harrison cautiously stood and took a deep breath. Gun held out, ready for action, he jumped over the books to the door. The short hallway was empty, and the door at the other end was closed. A quick search of the hallway outside the elevator told him that whoever it was had fled the scene.

Now the question is who, and how did he know I was here? I'd better call Tina. When people start coming out of the woodwork, firing guns at me, I must be onto something. But what?

Chapter Five

Tina Wolffe drove her bright red Honda Prelude cautiously along Van Ness, through the damaged city to Bay Street, past Moscone Center, toward Divisadero and Beach Streets. Katie Denton sat beside her in the passenger seat, dark sunglasses covering her green eyes. She wore Tina's green Giants baseball cap, her permed, flaming red hair tucked up under it in an attempt to keep her identity hidden from an, as yet, unknown killer, lurking somewhere in the devastated city.

A talk show host's voice from a local radio station filled the interior of the car with a deep, concerned tone. His guest was a seismologist from Stanford University. The two women listened with quiet curiosity as the guest spoke on the cause of the October 17th quake, and its epicenter near Los Gatos. They drove slowly past damaged buildings and the now homeless, evacuated citizens of the great city helping rescue workers search tirelessly through fallen buildings for victims buried beneath the rubble. An ambulance pulled away from the curb, its siren wailing; a signal that another rescue had been made.

The deep voice of the talk show host inquired of his guest, "So, have you pinpointed the exact epicenter of this killer quake?"

"Yes, Jack," the seismologist's excited voice answered in anxious anticipation, seemingly thrilled with the prospect of revealing his vital information, "A few miles west of Los Gatos, sixty miles or so, south of here. Officially, the quake is being named after the highest landmark near its epicenter, Loma Prieta, meaning dark hill."

"Was this the 'Big One', or could there be another, more devastating quake in our near future?"

"We're dubbing this one as the 'Pretty Big One', Jack. We believe that the 'Really Big One' is yet to come. It could come today or someday in the distant future; we really don't know."

Tina turned off the radio. Katie smiled nervously at her from behind the dark sunglasses. "Thanks. I really don't want to even think about another earthquake, let alone a bigger one."

"Yeah. So, they've named this quake, just like a hurricane; 'Dark Hill.' Seems appropriate somehow."

"I've been thinking about the quake," Katie pulled off her dark sunglasses and gazed ahead toward the Marina Yacht Harbor, with its hundreds of expensive water craft, anchored in a splendor that reflected the poshness of Marina District. Tina drove the bright red Prelude along Marina Boulevard, slowly past the harbor, contemplating the reasoning behind Brandon's call ten minutes earlier. He said to leave immediately and meet him in front of the Exploratorium at Divisadero and Marina. She barely heard Katie's reflection, but her passenger's voice demanded her attention somehow. "It hit at just the right time. It really saved my life by putting the killer off balance enough that he couldn't make sure I was dead."

"You're right! We know you're definitely being stalked. That's why we're out here." She checked the rear view mirror once again and scrutinized the light traffic behind them. Satisfied they weren't being followed, she executed the left turn in front of their destination and saw Brandon's silver Porsche 944 ahead, parked along the right curb, less than a block away.

Brandon was talking to Harry Garth, who was

leaning against the highly polished sports car. She knew that annoyed Brandon, but he didn't show the slightest contempt for Garth. He needed the police detective's help, she surmised.

Tina parked behind the 944. A smile came over Brandon's lips, a smile of both relief, and acknowledgment of her presence to Garth. She rolled down her green tinted window and watched the two men walk in front of the car and approach her. A nervous frown crossed Katie's red freckled face, as if she recognized the somber veteran police detective from an earlier, somewhat unpleasant confrontation.

Brandon smiled and gazed into Tina's dark Eurasian eyes. "Hi, sweetheart! Any problems getting here?" He glanced curiously at the uncomfortable looking passenger.

"No. Traffic was light and no buildings fell or crumbled around us." she said cheerfully.

"Well, I had a minor problem today. That's why I sent for you."

Garth bent down and peered into the car. He recognized Katie Denton immediately. "Hello, Miss Denton. You're in good hands. These two are the best in the business."

"At least they said they'd help! That's better than your department'll commit to." Her voice was low, with a noticeable scolding inflection, that caught him off guard.

"Yeah. Sorry about that. This earthquake's disrupted everything. With fires, looting and rescues, we don't have enough personnel to solve a murder now. I'm glad you took my advice and called on these two."

"Your advice, Harry?" Brandon was taken aback momentarily. He stared into the police detective's embarrassed, blue eyes, then smiled.

"Yeah. If I can't do the job, you're probably the best of the private sector."

"Why, thank you, Harry."

"Okay, don't get a big head over this. I merely told her to call you because I've known ya for so long."

"So, tell me about this minor problem," Tina opened the door and slid off the front bucket seat, then stood up into Brandon's arms. She gazed, questioningly, into his eyes, knowing that whatever had occurred must have to do with the present case. "Does it have to do with Katie?"

"I'm afraid so," he paused, as Katie got out of the car, closed the door and walked around the front of the red Prelude. She faced him, dark sunglasses hiding her curious green eyes. He turned to her, addressing comments to both women.

"What happened?"

"I stopped by your office a little while ago."

"And?"

"Someone took a couple of shots at me."

Tina gasped in horror, then grabbed his hand and faced him, concern and fear reflected in her eyes. "Are you all right?"

"Yes, he missed. My guess is that he didn't find what he was looking for at the time he killed Fisher. So, when he returned and found me snooping around, he got nervous."

"But why would he shoot at you? Why not just wait until after you'd left and then go in?"

"That's exactly the question I asked myself."

Tina stared down the street at a group of rescue workers digging through the still-smoldering debris of the one square block of apartment buildings, which had caught fire during the quake and burned to the ground. The air was thickly scented with a mixture of smoke rising from the smoldering piles of charred rubble, and the salty sea breeze, lightly blowing in across the marina less than a block away to the west. Her eyes returned to Brandon's concerned face.

"I want you to keep Katie out of sight today. You know, no public places." Brandon looked cautiously around the vicinity, eyeing a couple of passing cars which had driven by slowly, then had turned around after encountering the barricaded street, a block away.

"That'll be easy. Nothing's open anyway, except the 7-Eleven down the block. And there's a long line of people trying to get into it."

Brandon turned to Katie, who was looking down at the asphalt below her feet, as if in deep thought. She looked up into his eyes, removing the sunglasses that covered her anxious green eyes. "Katie? You say that you didn't remember turning off the lights of the office when you left on Tuesday."

"Umm... yeah." She thought about his statement momentarily. "I never turn 'em out. We leave that for the maintenance people to do."

"So, the lights were off in your reception area. You turned them on as you entered."

"Yes. It was almost dark in there."

"Now, after you got your bag out of the desk, you heard sounds in Fisher's office."

"Uh huh. I opened the door, and that's when I saw Dan."

"So the door was unlocked. That means at least one of them entered through the front door; probably Dan." She gazed up into his dark contemplative eyes as a slight breeze blew through his dark brown, medium length, wavy hair.

"Why just Dan?"

"I think the killer was waiting inside for him,

behind the locked door. He knew you'd gone after listening to you leave the message."

Harry Garth stepped beside Harrison and commented, "That'd explain the locked door and access by the killer, but why? Who had the motive? Come on, Harrison! You've gotta do better than this."

"Listen, Harry. I must've stumbled onto something. People just don't shoot at me for the hell of it." Irritated by the police detective's tone of voice, Brandon knew that he did have a point. He furrowed his brow in a frown, stared at Harry's ice-blue, triumphant eyes, then turned away and paced a few steps down the empty street.

The shrill sound of an ambulance siren signaled its passing along Marina Boulevard, with an urgency that alerted the surrounding community that another quake victim had been rescued. Tina walked over to her man and put her hand around his thick biceps. They watched the white emergency vehicle pass eastbound, toward the city.

"Weren't you able to find a clue in the office, an appointment calendar or a name on the desk?" Her voice was soothing, soft but compelling, forcing Brandon to focus his attention on the investigation instead of defending himself to Garth.

"As a matter of fact, he didn't have any calendars or notepads that I could see." He turned to Katie for confirmation of this observation.

"Dan never wrote anything down; maybe a note or two is about all. He kept his calendar in the PC, along with everything else. He and I have our own access code for each program. There must be several hundred dealings in the past couple of years since he opened."

"Can Tina or I use the computer?"

"Probably, but you wouldn't know where to

start. I can get anything you need out of it, fast." Katie's face gleamed with excitement, knowing she could help the investigation and possibly even find the answer to who murdered Dan.

"Wait a minute Harrison. There's a killer on the loose out there. I won't allow you to put her life in jeopardy by returning her to that office."

"Harry! We need her help. Send a couple men up there to support us. It'll only take a few minutes and it could give us other answers to your questions."

"I can't spare the manpower, but I'll come along," He walked away, a determined look on his face as he turned and caught sight of Brandon and Tina's triumphant, smiling faces. "I'm gonna let Black know where I'm going. I'll ride down with you, Harrison."

In a few short minutes, Garth and Harrison sped off in the silver 944, followed by Tina and Katie in the red Prelude. Traffic was still very light, allowing them to reach the Market Street Bay Building in less than ten minutes. Harrison determined that the safest place to park would be just outside the main entrance to the lobby, where Katie could be smuggled inside easily. The basement underground parking area would be darker, and heighten the possibility of an ambush if the murderer was in the building.

They entered the elegantly furnished lobby of the modern building. It was empty, with the exception of a security guard stationed at the front door. The youthful black man, dressed in a blue uniform, was armed only with a night stick, but was built with a six foot five stature that looked like he could handle any situation that might arise. He nodded to Garth, who flashed his badge, and they entered an awaiting elevator.

The ride to the tenth floor seemed, to Tina, to take entirely too long. Heights bothered her, and the numerous aftershocks of over 4.0 on the Richter scale didn't help the situation. The threat of one occurring while riding up ten stories in an elevator didn't appeal to her. Brandon put his arm around her petite waist and gently hugged her, reassuringly. "Are we almost there?" she whispered for his ear only.

"Halfway, honey."

After what seemed like an eternity to her, the elevator reached the tenth floor and its doors slid open. The office was midway down the quiet, well-lit hallway. Brandon checked his large, gold wristwatch as Katie inserted her key into the locked door and opened it. *Two thirty-six.*

Harry pulled out his .357 magnum revolver, then cautiously opened the door and peered inside the reception room. It was quiet, and seemingly undisturbed. He stepped inside, followed by Katie and Tina. Brandon drew his 9 mm Beretta, glanced both ways down the hall, and entered. He closed the door gently, turned the inside lock and switched on the office lights.

"At least we've got power," said Katie.

"Get to work on that while Harry and I take a good look around. Tina'll stay with you, right sweetheart?"

"You got it."

"Did you bring Ginger?"

She nodded, reached into her brown leather purse and brandished a black 9mm Beretta semiautomatic hand gun, identical to his.

"It's loaded and ready."

"Good," He smiled and touched her lips with his, then gazed confidently into her dark eyes, "Keep it handy. I don't want anything happening to either of you. I'll be in the next room with Garth."

A vibration shook the room momentarily beneath their feet, and the plants hanging from the ceiling in the corners swayed. "Just a small aftershock."

"I hate aftershocks," said Katie, nervously.

"Yeah. I just hope we don't have the 'Big One' while we're up here," said Tina. "Please hurry, okay Brandon?"

"I'll do my best."

Chapter Six

The occupants on the tenth floor of the Bay Building, high above Market Street, removed from the ongoing rescue and cleanup of the damaged San Francisco Bay area, couldn't hear the wailing sirens of ambulances and other rescue vehicles hasten below en route to nearby hospitals with newly discovered victims of the disaster.

Those who looked up from their tedious cleanup duties on the tenth floor and took the time to gaze out a window to the east, would see an unusual sight: an empty Bay Bridge. On closer inspection, one might see steel riggers and repair crews scrambling over the upper section of the expansive bridge that had taken a nose dive onto the lower level during the 7.1 quake.

Traffic had been light, as most commuters had left their respective jobs in order to be home by five to watch the World Series. Only one person had the misfortune of being on the bridge when that section collapsed. It crushed his car and abruptly ended his life.

Further east, cutting torches and cement saws crackled and whined, as rescue workers, military and police clawed through the mile and a quarter long pile of rubble of the Nimitz 880 freeway, in a last ditch effort to locate any more survivors still buried in their cars. With every aftershock, many measuring above 4.0 on the Richter scale, the danger of further collapse of the massive freeway structure posed a continual life-threatening situation for the rescue workers.

Oblivious to these outside events around the Bay area, Tina Wolffe and Katie Denton cleaned up the glass on the desk, reshelved a few books, then proceeded to retrieve the data stored on the floppy disks in the hopes of turning up a clue to Dan Fisher's murder. Katie's slender fingers rapidly worked the keyboard, while the printer rolled out laser copies for future analysis. Tina hadn't found any information that appeared to give the slightest hint of a suspicious nature.

"So far, we haven't really hit on anything. Try real estate."

Katie cleared the computer, pulled out the floppy disk, then inserted another. "This program'll show all of the real estate investments currently being handled by Dan. He was also involved in property management; mostly small apartment complexes. You know, up to twenty of our units."

"Can you bring them up on the screen?"

"No problem!" In moments, the current listing of seventeen addresses appeared on the screen, followed by the name and address of the owner, the square footage, the year built and other tax information which described each apartment complex.

Katie then printed out a hard copy of the information. A quick study of the data revealed one name that stood out as a major investor in twelve of the seventeen complexes: Jastrow Properties Inc. Tina's first thought of the find was that corporations usually have several controlling officers who hold most of the stock. "Do you have any information on the stock holders or board of directors for Jastrow Properties?"

Katie glanced up and stared questioningly into her dark, confident eyes. Tina managed a shrug of her shoulders and a little smile. "I know the board members. They're friends of mine and Dan's." She spoke in a surprised whisper, leaned back in her chair and waited for the PI's response.

"It's just routine. I've gotta check all possible leads, and these people could provide some information or insight to the murder."

Katie, with a pouting frown across her freckled face, brought up the file that would reveal the Jastrow Properties Inc, board of directors and its major stock holders. Tina continued her analysis of the property descriptions during the short process. Three properties, each an apartment complex, appeared to have been recently purchased by Jastrow within the last two months. The buildings had been constructed, in each case, during the early sixties.

The laser printer suddenly began spitting out the hard copy of the corporate executives. "Here's your printout," said Katie, nervously.

Tina leaned over her shoulder and began reading the blue computer. "Aron Jastrow, President; Richard Jastrow, Vice President of Property Procurement; Patricia Jastrow, Treasurer; Dan Fisher, Vice President of Property Administration; Michael Fallone, Vice President of Investments; Diane Lynn Jastrow, Secretary."

"They hold all one hundred percent of the stock."

"Equally?" Tina stared at the screen momentarily, then moved to the printer on the other side of Katie and removed the hard copy.

"Well... Aron and Richard own the controlling interest. Both own thirty percent."

"I see. And the rest of the stock is distributed between the remaining members?"

Katie stood beside her and pointed down at the sheet with her long, dark pink fingernail. "Pattie, Dan, Mike and Diane each own ten percent."

"So... Aron and Richard, are they brothers?"

"That's right. They have the money in the group, along with Pattie, who's Aron's wife. Diane's got a lot of money, too... but she has other pursuits besides real estate."

"Like?"

"She and Dan... they were gonna be married at Christmas," Katie's large green eyes misted over at the thought, and a tear rolled down each cheek. She turned and picked up the telephone receiver and punched in a number, "Poor Diane! I haven't called her yet. She's gotta know by now."

She listened as the phone rang several times, then hung up. Tina, puzzled by her action, watched curiously, formulating her next few questions while she patiently waited. "I take it that Diane's related to the Jastrows?"

"She's Aron and Rich's younger sister"

"I see. And who's Mike Fallone?"

Katie turned and walked to the door of Dan's inner office. She peeked inside. Harrison and Garth were not there. She stared down silently at the outline of Dan on the floor, then turned and walked back into her reception room, to the sofa directly across from the desk. "Mike was Dan's best friend. They'd known each other for years;

how many I don't know. He and Dan were in on the beginning of the corporation a few years ago."

"Any other information we should look at?" Tina asked. Her voice echoed her curiosity regarding the corporation as she read over the printout.

"Maybe the financial information on the corporation?"

"Can you give me that?"

"Sure." Katie smiled confidently, her green eyes beaming once more as she pulled out the floppy disk and inserted another. In a moment, she displayed the financial information on the monitor, then printed out a hard copy.

Tina tore the printout from the printer and stared down at it. "I'll have to analyze this thoroughly."

Brandon stepped through the doorway from the inner office. He had holstered his weapon. Tina smiled happily as their eyes met, then held out the printed copy to him. He took the white pages and leaned against the white secretary desk beside her.

"Financial information on Jastrow Properties. And the board of directors."

"Dan Fisher's partners in this venture," Her voice was low as she pointed to the names, trying to hide her excitement, "Look at these names!" "Interesting. What else have we got?"

"Here's the property the group's invested in and around the Bay area."

He scanned the printout while Tina leaned on his shoulder and re-read the list. "Did you get his appointment calendar out of this thing?"

"Right here, but it's really incomplete. It seems strange that he wouldn't jot down notes or have an appointment book of some kind, to refer to.

It's just unnatural."

"Yeah." Brandon took note of Tina's complaint while he looked over the printout on the investment properties. He raised his eyebrows and took out a pen from his shirt pocket, then circled an address. "Odd. This building, purchased this year, is pretty old. These others have been constructed within the last few years."

"How old is pretty old?"

"Sixty-five years," he said, without looking up from the readout.

Katie thought about his observation momentarily. Her intense eyes stared up at him from behind the computer, "But most of the apartment buildings in the city are that old... or older," she protested.

"That's right. I was merely making an observation about the age of these particular buildings, that's all."

Suddenly, Harry Garth stood at the door to the office. He leaned inside, a serious frown covered his face. "Harrison! Another body's been discovered on the next floor down."

Brandon looked up, startled by the revelation. He forced the printout into Tina's hand, then half ran across the reception room to join the police detective, who had turned and hurried down the hall toward the open elevator

Apprehensively, Tina watched her man leave, then stared momentarily into Katie's astounded eyes. They simultaneously felt a surge of adrenaline rush through their bodies at the realization that someone else had died. "Come on, we'd better go with them."

They ran out into the hall towards the elevator. Brandon happened to glance back to see them. "Hold it, Harry."

Quickly they jumped into the elevator, and in moments were on the ninth floor. The frightened look on Katie Denton's face told Brandon to expect that it could be a related death. The group rushed down the hall to #945 JASTROW PROPERTIES INC.

"Oh no!" Katie shrieked. "Please, God. It can't be!" Tina stopped before the door and held Katie from entering. "Tina, I've gotta go in and see who it is!"

"Well, okay, I guess so. Brandon?" She peeked through the door, then entered followed closely by Katie.

Brandon and Garth were standing behind the executive walnut desk, at the rear of the huge inner office. Two Chinese women of slight build, dressed in the blue cleaning uniforms of their company, sat on the plush, tan sofa along the far wall; one of the two was sobbing. Their faces were sober, frightened by the discovery they had made minutes earlier.

A San Francisco police officer, dressed in blue, stood up from behind the desk, revealing himself for the first time to Tina and Katie. "She's been dead for a couple of days. Shot through the heart, it looks like."

The two women made their way through the room, over a book-covered floor. The bookshelves that lined the walls behind the desk had emptied during the 7.1 quake. When they reached Brandon, Tina looked down at the body. It was completely covered with heavy law, property and investment books, telling her that the victim had been killed before the quake.

Katie stared down at the body, as Garth uncovered the head by removing several books. "God!" she sighed. Her face turned pale and a tear rolled down from her misty eyes. Her stomach tightened, "It's Sarah!"

Chapter Seven

The offices of Jastrow Properties Inc. suddenly became overcrowded. Arriving at the murder scene were four blue-uniformed, San Francisco police officers; three members of the lab team, two more detectives, including Phil Black, the coroner's department team and two reporters from the *Chronicle*. The usual crowd for a murder investigation.

Katie Denton sat with Tina on the reception room sofa, while the parade moved back and forth through the office. Katie had known Sarah Tulley over two years, since the first day of her employment. After welcoming Sarah to the office that day, she befriended, oriented, and helped train the petite, twenty year old blonde. She told Tina that Rich Jastrow had an eye for beautiful women. He only interviewed the prettiest applicants that applied. Each one had to have a high degree of developed office skills to qualify for an interview, but then Rich would choose and hire his favorite. That day, the lucky one was Sarah, and somehow she had lasted.

"Now she's dead." Katie wiped her eyes, and moaned with a deep sigh, "Why? How can this be? First Dan... now Sarah."

"I think it's probably the other way around, but I know what you mean." Tina gazed into her youthful yet saddened tear-filled eyes. Katie's anguished face reflected a fear that permeated her very soul, the fear and knowledge that whoever murdered Dan and Sarah was stalking her.

Suddenly, the door swung open beside them. An overweight, balding, fair-haired man, in his mid fifties, quietly stepped inside. He glanced around at the police in his office, then settled his excited green eyes on Katie. Aron Jastrow spoke softly in a deep voice to her. "Are you all right, Katie?"

She and Tina looked up at the well-dressed man in his conservative, gray suit. Then Katie sprang to her feet, into his arms and cried out desperately, "Oh, Aron! They've killed Sarah!"

"I know," Jastrow sighed, and rocked her gently in his arms, tears trying to force their way out of his eyes, "A Detective Garth called me a few minutes ago. I'm so sorry. First Dan..."

"Mister Jastrow?" Harry Garth peered through the doorway from the inner office, an emotionless, pure business look on his face.

"Yes," The response was low and barely audible to the police detective. Aron looked at him, then released Katie, "I'm Aron Jastrow. Are you Detective Garth?"

He nodded, then stepped into the room over a few scattered books, his badge held out in his left hand. "I've got a few questions for you. Can you come into your office with me? I'll need you to identify the body."

"Of course." He glanced into Katie's tear-filled eyes and whispered "This won't take long. I'll be right back." She smiled painfully, and resumed her seat beside Tina.

As the two men entered the inner office, a tall, youthful-looking man, hastily ran through the office door. With his blonde hair neatly combed back, the forty year old Richard Jastrow wore his usual pink sport shirt, beige slacks, and white sports coat. He didn't even glance at Katie and Tina on the sofa as he passed, but shouted loudly across the room to his brother.

"Aron! What's going on?" The three men disappeared into the office, leaving Tina to comfort

Katie alone. The two women looked at each other questioningly, then leaned back against the sofa.

Brandon Harrison glanced through the door at them, momentarily. "You all right, Tina? Katie?"

"Yeah, we're fine. Who's that guy in pink?"

"Richard Jastrow."

"Aron's brother," commented Katie, "They'll know what to do. They always do."

"I'm gonna sit in with Harry during questioning to see if I can get something, anything, for a lead."

"Good idea. We'll be okay."

Brandon smiled confidently, turned and strolled back inside. Katie looked to Tina and smiled weakly. "I've gotta go to the powder room. You want to come with me?"

They got up and left the office for the ladies' room across the hall. Several police officers were clustered in two groups on both ends of the tenth floor corridor. They all seemed to turn their heads at once and stare at Tina and Katie as they entered the ladies' room. The two women felt safe in their surroundings, safe from any threat of death, but not from the hungry eyes of their police guard.

Tina blushed and smiled in recognition of their stare, then pushed open the rest room door. Once inside, she held her hand back, signaling Katie to stop before going any further until she checked out the room. With six stalls as possible places for an assassin to lurk, she gingerly pulled her 9 mm handgun from her purse, then moved stealthily through the well-lit rest room.

The stalls were empty. There remained one door which apparently was a locked storage closet. She tried to open it, to no avail. Satisfied that it was safe, Tina motioned Katie inside. "I'll stand guard out here until you're done."

"If you think it's necessary. We do have our police protection just outside."

"Yeah, but nevertheless..." She smiled knowingly. Katie caught her satirical expression and agreed, then opened the door to the third stall and entered.

Tina dropped her leather purse next to the sink on the white-tiled counter. She gazed at her reflection in the mirror, which spanned the length of the counter, reached into the purse, found her dark pink lipstick, and smoothed it evenly over her beautifully shaped lips. Her gun lay beside the purse, where it was quickly retrievable, just in case.

Suddenly, she realized that a gun was pointing at her from inside the closet, the door slightly open. Her eyes had caught its reflection in the mirror. Adrenaline surged through her body in an instantaneous reaction.

In a heartbeat, she dove to the floor, fumbling for her gun in desperation. The mirror shattered when the two bullets exploded from the automatic. A terrifying scream echoed through the rest room from Katie's direction. Tina took aim as she bounced off the hard floor. She fired two shots into the door, the sounds of which reverberated in deafening explosions.

The two police officers who had been standing in the hall crashed through the rest room door, their guns leveled and ready for action. The first stared down at Tina on the floor, her gun pointed at the closet door. The second officer reached over to open it, but the handle was locked. He pulled on the door several times, but to no avail. Then he fired his weapon into the lock, splintering the wood around it. He yanked the door open and charged through.

Three more officers rushed inside as Tina got

to her feet, peered through the door momentarily, then frantically dashed back to the closed stall. Katie was curled up in a fetal position in the corner of the stall beside the toilet, her pants still down over her knees. "Katie?" Tina whispered afraid that she wouldn't respond.

"Tina!" She looked up, a terrified expression on her face.

"You're okay?"

Tina gave a sigh of relief when she realized that her charge wasn't dead.

"Shit. Did you get him?"

"No." Tina reached down and grasped her hand. Katie pulled herself up, then looked down, embarrassed that her pants were down. She pulled them up. Brandon anxiously appeared in the stall behind Tina.

He saw the jagged bullet holes that had ripped through the metal portions that divided the three stalls, lodging in the plaster wall, behind the toilet where Katie had sat moments before. "That was close!"

"Brandon, how did he know?" said Tina.

"I don't know. Stay with Katie. I'm gonna try to find out!" Quickly, he turned and entered the hallway through the door. Glancing toward the end, about twelve feet away, Harrison saw two office doors on either side. The doors were both open, with a couple of police officers investigating within the confines of those suites.

"Whoever it was had to go into one of those offices," Harry Garth stepped through the doorway from the women's room, followed by Tina and Katie, "I've got men going through them now. He won't get off this floor."

"Let's check the hall and elevator," countered Brandon.

He hastily brushed past Garth, through the open door into the tenth floor hallway. To his dismay, the PI was confronted by a crowd of probably, twenty curious spectators. He stopped dead in the doorway, with Tina nearly pushing him on through, as she tried to stop abruptly behind him.

They stared at the crowd momentarily, then frowned into each other's surprised eyes. "So he won't get outta here, huh Harry?"

Brandon scanned the faces of the crowd. Aron and Richard Jastrow were among the first that he made contact with. The two brothers pushed their way through to him as Katie stepped forward, past Tina and into Aron's arms.

Tina walked slowly into the crowd, her hand still clutching "Ginger", tightly in her purse. She moved cautiously along the hall, toward the elevator, where a group of bystanders were waiting. The door slid open and the group, almost simultaneously, moved quickly inside.

A man in a dark suit kept his back to them, his face behind the others, peering down at the floor. Nervously, he stepped inside, not once looking up, as he entered the elevator.

The door closed as Brandon reached the elevator. His hand stretched out and hit the lighted 'Down' button on the wall several times, but to no avail. The door remained closed and the elevator moved down through the building.

Suddenly, the doors on the elevator to their right, opened. After a quick glance into each other's eyes to confirm the next move, the two stepped inside, closed the door and hit the button for 'Garage'.

Chapter Eight

"Do you think that was the murderer?" Tina stood taut against the back wall of the moving elevator. Staring up at the bright numbers above the door, she watched as they counted down.

Brandon looked thoughtfully into her suspense-filled eyes, "Call it a hunch. He's the guy. He crammed into an elevator jammed with people. He tried to keep his back to us to conceal his face."

"Shit! He almost killed Katie, and me!"

Their car slowed to a stop and the door slid open on the sixth floor. Several people anxiously waited to enter. Brandon pulled his wallet from the inside breast pocket of his sport coat, and flashed a silver police badge at the group, "Police, please don't enter. Wait for the next elevator."

He pushed the 'Close Door' button, and the doors slid shut. Confidently, he smiled at Tina and they continued their descent. She giggled girlishly at his impersonation, then wrapped her arm around him and pulled herself close. "Clever, Brandon. But how do you know that he's heading for the garage?"

"Escape... that's his main drive now."

Suddenly, the elevator car shook under their feet. A loud, growling sound rumbled up through the elevator shaft. Tina felt her stomach squeeze and tighten. Her arms tightened their hold around her man. The lights flickered off momentarily. The elevator jolted and shut down for one frightening second. "Oh, shit, Brandon! We're trapped!"

Suddenly, the lights flickered on and it started to move once again.

"That was bad." Brandon stared into her frightened eyes, then hugged her with his strong arms.

"God, I hate earthquakes," she sighed, and loosened her grip on his arm. Seconds later, the car came to a gentle halt at their destination; the garage.

The dimly lit parking level was full of shadows, because most of the florescent lighting was off.

Brandon pulled his Beretta out from under his sport coat. Cocking it in preparation for a possible confrontation, he took Tina by the hand. The two stepped out of the bright elevator car and into the shadowy garage. Carefully, they moved toward the elevator to their right. Apparently they had beaten it down. Tina felt her weapon, still gripped tightly in her hand.

At the extreme right end of the garage, the dull light from an overcast sky shone through the main auto exit. A car was pulling out onto Market Street. Brandon hoped it wasn't their quarry, then realized it couldn't be.

Cautiously, Harrison led the way to a point in the dark beyond the elevator. It took only moments for the doors to slide open. Three riders stepped out, two women and a man. None of them were their suspect. They all seemed somewhat unsure about where their cars were parked. Each person cautiously eyed the two PI's in passing, a touch of anxiety in their steps.

"That's it then, Brandon." Tina shrugged.

He started toward the open doors. Suddenly, a black automatic handgun, held by someone against the wall inside, poked out at him.

"Brandon!"

He hit the floor, then rolled. A burst of deadly fire blasted from it in loud, furious explosions. Tina instantly retaliated, blasting three rapid shots that ripped through the stainless steel elevator wall. She dove for cover behind a thick concrete column. The killer's bullets missed her, crunching into the trunk of a nearby parked car.

The deafening roar of Brandon's gun filled the garage, as it spewed out two more shots into the closing door. The elevator lifted, taking the assassin away. Harrison jumped to his feet. Swiftly, he raced past Tina, opened the stairway door to their right, then turned to her, "Wait here and watch the elevator."

Quickly, he traversed the stairs three at a time, then burst through the door into the lobby. Harry Garth stood facing him. Brandon pushed past the police detective and ran towards the elevator.

"Harrison, what's going on?

"Did anyone get out of that elevator just now?" The lighted numbers above the door indicated its upward movement past the fourth floor, then the fifth. Harrison watched in anxious anticipation until the elevator stopped on the eighth floor.

Garth joined him at the closed, stainless steel door, "It didn't even open here," He realized at once Brandon's concern. "Don't worry. Your client's safe down here. They're in the security office over here. What the fuck happened?"

"Our man was in the elevator. We exchanged some hot lead down on the parking level."

"Shit! Harrison." Harry Garth glared at him, his voice hostile with anger. "Another shoot-out? Damn it, Brandon, why's there always gunplay when you're involved?"

"It wasn't my idea! He opened fire on us."

"Yeah? Did you get a look at him?"

"No." The two men stood face to face.

Suddenly, Tina burst through the stair door, glanced at Brandon, and ran over to his side, knowing that their quarry had escaped by the look on her man's face. She reached out and pressed the lighted down button, to bring the elevator down. "I don't know if we hit him, but it's possible."

"All right. Tell me about it, Tina."

"Didn't Brandon?"

"I wanna hear it from you."

Harrison shrugged, then turned to watch the numbered lights flash above the elevator door, as it descended once again. Several uniformed officers surrounded them to await its arrival. Tina got a doubtful nod from Brandon, then turned to Garth, "I just fired a few rounds into the elevator when, whoever it was, started shooting at us." She turned away from Garth and stood beside Brandon in innocent defiance.

"That's it? You put a few holes in private equipment and that's all you can say? Shit!"

"What'd you want me to do, Harry? Just stand there and let him kill us?" Her dark eyes pierced his. Her anger and frustration was building. "I don't understand you, Harry. Some crazy's out there shooting at us and all you can think about is what it's gonna cost the department!"

Harry grunted, then paced impatiently in front of the elevator door. "Okay, okay. I get the point. I guess I'm just mad because we blew it and let this guy get away."

Tina grabbed Brandon by the arm and turned him toward the security office, across the front lobby. The elevator door opened. Garth ordered several of his men to search the eighth and ninth floors, and evacuate the people up there for their protection.

The PI's hurried through the lobby to Building Security, where Katie Denton and the Jastrow brothers waited. Katie sat between the two men. A strained silence settled over them as they awaited news of the capture of the assailant.

Garth led them into the office, past two blue uniformed officers. The disappointed frown on Harrison's face and in Tina's expression said it all to the three occupants.

"Tina! Brandon! Did you get him?" Katie jumped up, unable to contain her need to know what was happening.

"No. He got away," Brandon replied. "Now, let's get you out of here while we've got a chance. We're gonna have to find a safe place to keep you until this is over."

"She can stay with me," said Aron Jastrow. "I live in a secure home, with round-the-clock guards and a full security system."

"Or at my place," Richard Jastrow stood up and stepped between Aron and Brandon. "There's no safer environment in San Francisco."

Katie looked at him, then at Aron. "I don't think I'd be very safe with you, Richard. As for you Aron, your wife, Patricia, probably wouldn't approve."

"She wouldn't mind if..."

"It's okay, Katie,' interrupted Tina. "We'll make the arrangements. Now, let's get going."

A shuffling sound at the door outside, distracted the group. They turned to see a handsome,mustached man enter, escorted by a police officer. "Shit... don't push! I didn't do anything! What's going on?"

"Harry... we found this guy on the ninth floor, suspiciously sneaking around."

"Mike!" exclaimed Katie in recognition.

"This is Mike Fallone, one of our associates," said Aron.

"What's going on, Aron? Are the police finally investigating Dan's death?"

"We've had more problems here."

Harry Garth interrupted their conversation, stepping between Fallone and Aron. "What are you doing here?"

"I came up to see if I could help put the office back together, at Richard's request. Tell 'em, Richard."

"I'm afraid he's telling the truth. I needed him to get the office back in order so we could resume business. I've got a lot of buildings out there. We've got to get the insurance claims going so repairs can be initiated."

As Katie smiled meekly at Mike, tears began to trickle down her cheeks. She stammered trying to tell him about the events of the morning, "Mike... Sarah's dead."

"Dead?" He looked in shock at her, then saw Aron and Richard nod in agreement. "How? When? I..."

Brandon watched this new player in the scenario, wondering where he fit into the picture. He heard Garth explain the circumstances of how she had been found and the attempts on Katie's life.

"You don't think I had anything to do with this?"

"Everyone's a suspect at this point. Jack, you can take the cuffs off him."

The uniformed officer released the handcuffs from Michael Fallone's hands, then departed. "I'm gonna need statements from all of you before we leave," said Harry. "Brandon, Tina, take her out of here and contact me later."

"Right."

Aron stepped forward and grasped Katie's hand. "Are you going to attend the services and the funeral for Dan tomorrow?"

"Yes. I'll be there." She turned and walked into the lobby with Tina and Brandon. They stopped at the glass doors and he turned to Katie, a serious look covering his face.

"I don't think it's a good idea for you to attend the funeral."

"Why? I have to. Dan was my friend for a long time."

"It could be too dangerous."

"I don't care. I'm going, like it or not. Tell him, Tina. I have to go!"

"I agree with Brandon, it could be dangerous. But if you have to go..."

"I don't care, I'm going!"

Tina shrugged and Brandon opened the door. "The funeral it is. But for now, we've gotta find a safe place to keep you for the night. There's still a killer out there somewhere, stalking you."

Chapter Nine

"Will we be safe here tonight, Tina?" Katie Denton asked. She stood in front of Tina's large bay window, in the living room of the recently constructed condominium, staring out at the view of San Francisco's Golden Gate Bridge. It stood relatively unscathed by the disaster of two days earlier, a monument of the strength and courage of the City by the Bay. Bright, scant, rays of sunlight pierced the dark storm clouds to the west , then filtered over the magnificent bridge. It appeared to shine with a luminescence that covered the entire bridge, reaffirming its name.

"Yes. Make yourself at home."

A lush, tree-filled park occupied the immediate foreground, which was the Presidio Golf Course, a major portion of the Golden Gate National Recreation Area. To the west was Baker Beach and the Pacific Ocean, extending out as far as the eye could see. A massive supertanker appeared on the horizon, heading for a port in the bay.

Katie Denton stood in silent awe, watching the bridge in the distance, taking in the whole splendid view. It was five p. m. Exactly forty eight hours since her ordeal had begun. She watched Tina pick up a photograph of her and Brandon, taken somewhere in the redwoods, from the floor behind her television. Tina replaced it atop the T.V, then frowned slightly with a glance around the living room.

"There! That takes care of that. The earthquakes haven't damaged much here. I guess these newer buildings are built to take them."

"Yeah. I wonder how my apartment did."

"Haven't you been home yet?"

"No, I'm afraid to. I went to my girlfriend's and borrowed some clothes to wear. I had some other clothes in my car. I picked it up after I left the hospital." Katie paced before the large bay window, anxiety etched on her girlish face. Reaching Tina's favorite rocking chair, she eased herself down into it, and sat in stiff silence.

Tina watched her dismayed client momentarily, knowing from experience what she had to be going through. A few strained seconds of silence filled the room before she decided to check the refrigerator. Most of the food would probably be bad, having gone without electricity for so long, but she figured that the fruit and canned drinks should be okay.

Within a couple of minutes, she carried a tray of sliced apples, peaches, melon, grapes and two bottles of cherry flavored Calistoga water.

"You hungry?"

Katie looked up at her host, a faint smile crossing her lips, "Sure, looks good."

"It's all I've got left that wasn't spoiled. I hope Brandon brings something when he gets here."

"Where'd he go?"

"Back to his house to pick up a few things for the night."

"I'm glad I don't have to spend another night alone. I feel much safer with you and Brandon around. Last night I slept in my car, in front of the police station! I didn't get any sleep, really. I was too afraid. I know I'll be safe here."

"Yes, we'll be fine here. No one can get in except by the front door, and he'd have to come up two flights of outside stairs. The patio is two floors up and impossible to climb up to."

Katie relaxed her stiff body, took a bottle from Tina and took a sip. "I thought you two lived together. Obviously, I was wrong."

"Not completely. I keep my condo because sometimes I need some private space. You know, to be alone."

"No, I'm not sure what you mean."

"Well, I don't need it so much anymore. I got it two years ago when I moved here from Eureka. Now it's mainly a place to keep my furniture. I do practically live with Brandon. I guess it's silly to keep, but it's an investment, too."

"You're lucky. Maybe someday, Bobby and I will be that close," She remembered her boyfriend and how she hadn't seen him for four days. There had been no time, and no way to contact him. With phone service out and the Bay Bridge closed, she couldn't reach him in Berkeley. "Can I use your phone?"

"Sure, if it's working."

Katie's eyes lit up with anticipation of talking to her boyfriend. Tina showed her the phone in the den, just off the living room, and left her to talk in privacy with her friend. She knew Katie had made contact when girlish giggles emanated from the den.

Tina smiled to herself, then slipped a C.D. into the compact disc player. The smooth jazz sounds of Sade, *Promise,* filled her home as she picked up little odds and ends which had fallen from the shelves. She then cleaned and dusted her living room furniture.

Fifteen, twenty minutes went by, then a half hour, and still the girlish giggles from the den that cheerfully echoed through the condo. Tina stepped outside through the French doors onto the patio. The sunset glowed orange and yellow hues around billowing storm clouds to the west. Another storm was imminent that night, but it looked beautiful on the horizon.

The familiar sound of Brandon's Porsche caught her attention, as he drove into the parking lot below. He tapped the horn twice before pulling into the garage below her unit.

In a second, Brandon appeared at the bottom of the stairs, carrying two large bags of groceries under his arms. Quickly he ran up the stairs, taking them two at a time.

Tina opened the front door just as he made it to the top landing. Brandon looked back at the parking lot with a cautious eye, scanned the area for a quick second look, then entered. "How're you doing, love?" He smiled his warm, charming smile, put the bags on the table, then gazed into her eyes and tenderly touched his lips to hers.

"I'm okay. Katie's been talking on the phone to her boyfriend for quite a while."

"Her boyfriend?" She nodded and glanced at the den. He smiled, then drew her close with his strong, confident hands. Their lips touched in sensual unity. He gently stroked her long, black hair and ran his hands tenderly down her back. Tina drew him close, feeling a heated passion that filled her body with desire, and an intense need to make love to him. But she knew she'd have to wait.

A door opened adjacent to them. Katie walked out of the den and uttered a faint sound of surprise. Tina hesitantly drew away from her Brandon. "I didn't mean to interrupt, but I've invited my boyfriend, Bobby, over tonight. I hope it's all right?"

Brandon stared into Tina's eyes, a dismayed look on his face, and shrugged his shoulders. Tina smiled, then giggled and turned to Katie. "Of course it is. Do you need an address and instructions?"

"No, I already told him how to find the condo. I took good mental notes on the way. Oh, and he's gonna bring pizza. He said the Red Baron's open. He'll pick up a couple along the way."

Brandon grinned as he picked up the groceries from the table and carried them to the spacious kitchen. "I guess we won't need this stuff tonight. When's your friend gonna get here?"

"In an hour or so." Katie said, following Tina to the kitchen. She watched her hosts put away the food that Brandon had just purchased. A look of wonder crossed her face at the amount of food he had put into those two bags. "It looks like you're prepared for another seven point earthquake."

"We may have to stay a couple of days," said Tina. "The killer knows where Brandon lives."

"Yeah? I thought we might have to stay for awhile, so I asked Bobby to stop by my apartment. He's gonna pick up some extra clothes for me."

"You what?" Brandon looked into her eyes, an anxious look of disbelief covered his face. "Call him back now! Tell him not to go there."

"But, Brandon..."

"I'm sorry, but if the killer sees him... just get on the phone, Katie."

"You're right! I'm sorry!" Katie rushed into the den and dialed the number. The phone at the other end rang and rang, as she held the receiver to her ear. It was ten, eleven, then twelve rings before Katie hung up. She dialed once more to make sure she'd dialed correctly. The phone rang several more times.

Finally, Katie gave up and turned to Brandon, who was standing with Tina in the doorway, "He's gone." She sighed with an apologetic tone, her face weary and covered with guilt.

"Call the Red Baron Pizza House," suggested Tina. "Maybe we can stop him."

"Which one?"

"Golden Gate Park, but he'll probably go by my place first."

"Maybe. But we've gotta try to cut him off." Brandon said. He thumbed through the yellow pages, found 'Pizzas', and dialed the number. "What's his name?"

"Mason."

The phone rang at the other end. A cheery woman's voice answered "Red Baron, may I help you?"

"Yes. We ordered a pizza a while ago, for Bob Mason. When he picks it up, could you have him call Katie? We need him to get a couple more things."

"Okay, will do." Brandon gave her Tina's number, thanked her, then hung up.

"What can we do now?" Katie looked at him with questioning eyes.

"Not much but wait," replied Tina.

"You two stay here. I've gotta go out to your apartment, Katie, just in case he goes there first. Give me your keys and your address."

"Oh, Brandon! Don't let anything happen to him." Katie's eyes reflected her fear as she handed him the keys. After a brief explanation of the location of her apartment complex, Brandon departed. Tina and Katie watched from the window high above the parking lot while he pulled out of the garage.

He looked up at the window, waved, and drove to the street. *Why can't anything be easy? Why does it always have to get so complicated?* He checked the street both ways, pulled out his gun, placed it on the passenger seat, then floored the gas pedal. The Porsche 944 sped away with a powerful roar.

Chapter Ten

Harrison found Katie Denton's apartment building on Sunset Boulevard with relative ease. After locating her apartment upstairs on the north end, he decided to station himself inside his car in the parking lot. He would be in full view of Katie's front door and the entrance to the parking area. *Her boyfriend'll have to pass me, if he comes at all.*

From that vantage point, he watched several cars drive in and out of the parking lot, carefully scrutinizing the occupants of each vehicle. The tenants hurried into the shelter of their apartments, carrying bags of groceries and briefcases; a sign that the city was beginning to recover from the disaster of two days earlier.

Through the dark and the rain, he watched. Still no one approached Katie's apartment. He waited a half an hour, then figured it would take her friend at least another thirty minutes or more, in the rain and traffic , to cross the Richmond Bridge to the north and travel down 101, to Katie's. *He may not even arrive if he got the message at Red Baron, but that isn't the point of the stakeout.*

Carefully, he scrutinized the premises for anyone just hanging around the complex. He had just decided to get out and stretch his legs, when a late model, red pickup truck pulled into the lot and stopped in front of the apartment building. *Hello! What've we got here?*

The truck drove to the end of the lot, turned around and cruised past, slowly. Suddenly, the sky opened up, unleashing a heavy rain, covering Harrison's windshield with a flood of water that cascaded down the glass. He dared not turn on the wipers, so he reached over and rolled down the passenger window. As the pickup truck drove slowly by, he took a mental note of the license plate number.

The truck reached the street. Brandon opened the car door, slid out, grabbed his gun, then stealthily ran behind the parked cars, toward the exit. His suspect turned right. Within moments, he reached the street, but the truck was gone. "What the hell? Where'd it go?" Several cars approached from the east, but to the west there were only tail lights of four cars, none of which were pickups.

He raced up the sidewalk through the rain to a residential street of older apartment buildings. The truck was gone. Harrison thought better of walking down the dark street in search of it. Instead, he decided it would be more prudent to make his way back into the complex and find a place where he could keep an eye on the apartment at close range, and get out of the pouring rain. *If that was the guy, he'll probably come over the fence at the end the parking lot, or wait there for someone to enter Katie's before acting.*

The apartment directly opposite hers appeared to be empty and unoccupied. The curtains were pulled wide open behind each of the three windows facing the walkway at the top of the stairs. He drew out his favorite lock pick from an inside pocket, pulled the collar of his soaked sports coat up around his neck, and climbed the stairs

Reaching the door, he had a quick look around for anyone approaching, then quickly picked the lock as if he were using a key. The apartment was totally vacant.

Quickly, he closed the curtains, engulfing the room in darkness. The curtain on the window that faced Katie's apartment was left parted for an easy view of her door. He slid the front window open slightly, and listened quietly in the dark for a moment, then removed his wet coat and hung it next to the kitchen doorway.

He waited.

There were only four apartments upstairs, in Katie's group. Only two others were occupied, besides hers. That meant that traffic up the stairs should be light. It was. After almost a half hour, someone ran up the stairs. *A man, dark hair, probably in his mid-twenties.* He was dressed in Levi's jeans, with a dark blue, wool sweater, and white tennis shoes. He stopped at Katie's door.

The moment he went inside the apartment, Harrison opened the door and slipped across the walkway, then entered right behind him, gun in hand. Shoving the man inside, he kicked the door closed. In an instant, the man turned on him, lashing out with a right hook, that connected with a heavy blow to Harrison's jaw.

The P.I. stumbled back. Instantly he regained his footing. A powerful blow of a left upper cut to the man's stomach, sent him doubled up and sprawling backwards, onto the carpeted floor. He cried out in pain as his head hit the floor.

Harrison aimed his gun down at him and switched on the light. He grinned at the captive. "Bobby Mason, I presume?" The man stared up at him, grimacing in pain and fear.

He nodded, "Who are you? What'd you want?" He struggled to his feet.

Brandon holstered his weapon and closed the door. "Harrison. Brandon Harrison, private investigator. Katie Denton sent me to find you. Sorry about that. Are you okay?"

Mason eased back onto the pillows on the mauve-colored sofa, still looking up at Harrison with uncertainty. "Yeah, I think so. Why'd you come here? What's going on?"

"We tried to reach you at the pizza place, to stop you from coming to Katie's apartment."

"I haven't been there yet! Anyway, what's going on?"

"Katie's in very real danger. If the person who killed her boss is out there..."

Bobby Mason stood up suddenly, in astonishment. "He could be out there? Why?"

"Because he's tried for Katie three times. I don't want to alarm you, but you're in danger just being here." He paused, turned and locked the door, then walked over to the curtained window. Standing beside the television, he pulled the curtain out slightly, and scanned the parking lot for any sign of danger. "I should send you back to Berkeley..."

"No! I need to be with her!"

"Keep your voice down." Harrison continued to peer outside for a few moments, then turned to him, "It'll be too dangerous sending you back home. He may follow you to get to Katie."

"I'll be able to help. What can I do?"

"Pack up some things for her, as she asked. We'll use my car and leave yours here."

"Right! I'll be ready in a minute!" Mason quickly packed the clothing, as requested by Katie. Harrison retrieved his coat from the apartment across the way, keeping an eye out for trouble.

Then, together, the two men made their way down the stairs, across the parking lot, through the rain, and climbed into the Porsche. Harrison started the car and drove slowly out of the parking lot to Sunset Boulevard, which was relatively quiet for that time of the evening, with only light traffic in either direction.

He kept a cautious eye on the rear view mirror as he pulled out into the street, traveling east and away from Tina's condo. A pickup truck pulled out behind them from the street past the apartment complex. Brandon wasn't sure who it was, but it was no time to ask questions.

"Shit! We may have a problem." He quickly shifted into third, and rapidly accelerated to put distance between them.

The light turned red just ahead. He swerved into the right lane in front of a large white sedan, skidding into a sharp right turn as the cars at the opposite corner started. They sped off south, as the rain continued to pound down harder.

The pickup truck swung onto the street two blocks behind them. "We're being followed, all right."

Bobby Mason turned to see the lights behind them."Is that why you're driving crazy like this?"

"Yeah hold on. We're going for a fast ride." Brandon smiled conspiratorially at Mason, then turned left with a quick touch of the wheel. His foot nailed the pedal to the floor, and the Porsche flew up the dark street. He whipped the wheel right and sped down the next quiet street several blocks, then turned left and slowed.

"That should lose him. Now we can get on to Tina's condo."

Brandon's passenger breathed a deep sigh of relief. His knuckles were white from holding on so tight to the dashboard, fearful that they would crash at any moment during their flight.

The drive back to Tina's condo passed without any further incident. Ten minutes later, they pulled into her garage, parked and ran up the stairs. Tina opened the door, and they rushed inside.

"Bobby!"

"Katie! Are you okay?"

"I'm all right. Did you bring the pizza?"

"No, we couldn't. Someone was following us! Tell 'em, Brandon."

Harrison frowned, "Do you two know anyone with a red pickup?"

"Several people," said Bobby. "But I didn't get a good look at the one that followed us. What a wild ride, Katie! I had to leave my car at your place."

Brandon turned to Bobby and Katie, then paced momentarily to the bay window overlooking the parking lot.

"What's the matter?" said Tina

He looked at the couple. "Did you bring the address and directions with you, Bobby?"

"Why, yes..." He put his hands into his pockets in search of the piece of paper he had recorded Katie's instructions on earlier. "Oh, no. I left them on the front seat of my car."

"Oh, great," Brandon mumbled. He gazed into Tina's knowing eyes, then walked into the kitchen and dialed the phone.

"Who you calling?" Tina asked.

"Harry. Maybe he can get a car out there before it's too late."

Chapter Eleven

Friday morning brought a dark onslaught of heavy rain with the major storm front that blew in from the Pacific Northwest overnight. Harrison slept restlessly during the night. The harsh, howling winds outside the secure condo created all sorts of mysterious sounds; sounds which were impossible to differentiate from.

Restless, he lay awake most of the night in the darkness of the living room, in anticipation of a possible attack by their murderous stalker. Tina, on the other hand, slept through the storm, waking only once to find Brandon sitting alone in the dark.

At three a.m., a tremendous gust of wind shook the building, like a sharp earth tremor. It jolted Tina awake from a relatively deep sleep. She found that Brandon was not beside her. Throwing on her warm robe, she crept into the living room to find his shadowy shape, barely discernible in the almost total,darkness, lying on the sofa.

"Brandon?" she whispered. Moving carefully through the darkness, Tina sat down beside him on the edge of the pillow. His hand tenderly touched hers. "Come to bed with me, okay?"

"I'd better stay put here, my love. I don't wanna take any chances tonight. Our man may know where we are, and if that's the case..."

"If that's the case, then move over." She leaned gracefully over his chest, brushed her lips to his, and laid her body over Brandon.

"There's more room on the floor," he said.

Tina smiled seductively. She sat up, straddling his hips, and unbuttoned his shirt. "Yeah, but don't you like tight places?"

He gazed into her dark, beautiful eyes as she

pulled his shirt off from under him. She leaned forward, kissed his bare, hair-covered chest, moving her hips slowly over him in sensual rhythm. He responded. Aroused by her sexual advance, Brandon lightly caressed Tina's body with strong, but gentle hands.

The lovers, in an urgent heat of lust and passion, disrobed each other with quiet ease. The heavy breathing of sexual desire while they kissed was the only sound that mattered to Brandon. The fierce storm raged over the city through the night, while inside they created their own love-filled storm on the sofa, in the dark.

Sunrise filtered through the curtained windows over the two lovers lying quiet and happy in each other's arms. Tina opened her eyes slightly to greet the morning, and found Brandon gazing sleepily at her. She smiled, then touched his lips with hers, in a light, soft kiss. "Let's go to bed for a while," she whispered.

"Yeah," He moved slightly, in a feeble attempt to vacate the sofa, but she held him in place with her legs wrapped snugly around him. "So you'd rather stay here?"

She giggled a soft, girlish laugh. Their lips met once again in warm passion, as their bodies moved together in a slow, sensual rhythm.

Suddenly, Brandon sprung up and away from her, grabbed his gun from the coffee table beside them, and leapt to the window. Pulling the drape back slightly, he peered outside. Someone was standing at the bottom of the stairs.

Tina, startled by his actions, quickly jumped up and ran down the hall to her bedroom. She reappeared instantaneously, in her flowered robe, her 9 mm in hand. She ran to Brandon's side, then peered outside. "Who is it?"

"I can't tell. Watch him while I get dressed." Brandon pulled on his pants, then his shirt. In moments he was fully dressed. Tina strained to identify the man, whose back was to them. "What's he doing?" Brandon asked.

She watched, then in a moment of recognition as he turned slightly, Tina knew. "Harry!"

"Harry Garth?" He pulled the drapes apart slightly more, and smiled. "So it is."

"How'd you know someone was out there?"

"I heard his footsteps on the stairs."

Tina walked to the front door and opened it. Harry looked up, smiled and gave a short salute, then proceeded up the stairs. "Good morning." His voice was low, but cheerful.

Brandon confronted the police detective when he walked inside. "All right, Harry. What're you doing up so early, standing guard on the condo?"

"I figured you'd see me out there sooner or later. Got any coffee?"

"Coming right up," replied Tina.

"The car was broken into. No address or instructions on how to get here." Harry spoke in a low, warning tone. The two men stared at each other disconcertedly, each knowing exactly what the implications meant. Tina stopped momentarily in the kitchen as she caught the ominous warning.

"Well, so much for a safe place to stay. I guess we'll just have to break this thing wide open today."

Harry grinned and nodded. "Got any leads?"

"Just the red Toyota pickup. Did ya run that license through DMV?"

"Got someone on it now. The lines are down all over, so we've been unable to get through. I should have it this morning sometime, but it's probably a stolen vehicle."

"What about this Michael Fallone, the partner you rounded up in the Bay Building?"

"Fallone's checked out. He's clean. Aron Jastrow asked him to come to the offices and begin cleaning up the place."

"And the Jastrows?"

"Clean, as far as I can determine."

"No skeletons in the closet? No law suits pending? Any enemies?"

"The department hasn't been able to determine the answers to those questions, Harrison. All we know is they haven't got a record."

"There's a lot of things that don't make sense." Brandon said, walking slowly toward the kitchen. Tina had just pulled the coffee from the microwave. She handed him two full cups over the breakfast bar, then took hers and sauntered into the dining room and sat at the round, wooden table. Brandon and Harry joined her.

Tina sipped on her hot coffee, a thoughtful look of contemplation in her deep brown eyes. "What was the killer looking for? It looks like whatever it was, he didn't find it in Aron Jastrow's office."

"Maybe he did find it in Jastrow's office."

Tina and Harry looked up from their coffee curiously at Brandon. "You mean Sarah Tulley?"

"Possibly. After killing her, the murderer proceeded up to Dan Fisher's office and shot him."

"But why? I need a motive."

"And, Brandon, why is this killer stalking Katie? That doesn't make sense."

"Whoever it is thinks that she might be able to identify him, or her."

"Or her?" Tina sat back in her chair, sipped on her coffee and thought for a moment. "It has to be a man."

"Why do you say that?"

"Well, Katie said his strong hands picked her up and pushed her into the elevator. She always refers to the killer as he. A woman knows when she's being handled by a man, Brandon."

"She's got a point, Harrison."

A door opened down the hall and Katie appeared. She smiled sleepily, and went into the bathroom. Bobby Mason soon followed, fully dressed in the same clothes he'd been wearing when he arrived. He took a seat at the table, cautiously eyeing the police detective.

"Good morning," said Brandon. "Bobby Mason, meet detective Harry Garth, of the San Francisco Police Department. Bobby is Katie's friend."

Bobby reached out over the table and shook Harry's hand, limply. "Anything wrong, sir?"

"You might say that. Brandon asked me to keep an eye on your car. By the time we got there, it'd been broken into. The door was left wide open. There were no visible scratches on the doors to show it was broken into. Did you leave it unlocked?"

"I don't remember, but it's possible. We were in a hurry to leave, and I didn't lock it when I went upstairs to Katie's. I guess I didn't lock it."

Katie Denton appeared from the bathroom, dressed only in a pink negligee one could practically see through. Her dark red hair was brushed back in permed waves, and hairsprayed. Even without makeup, which she wore sparingly, her youthful beauty was stunning. "Good morning, everyone. Hi, Bobby." She said as she strolled over to her man's side.

Harry smiled enviously, unable to keep his eyes from staring at the outline of her body beneath the fragile nightgown. Tina knew that her man had a rough time of it too, but smiled and stepped into Brandon's arms, gently reminding him of her presence. "Like a cup of coffee, you two?"

"Yes. I'd love one," said Katie. She sat beside Bobby, who declined with a slight shake of head. "What's the matter?"

"I left my car unlocked at your apartment."

"So?"

"So, somebody got the directions and Tina's address you gave me off of the front seat." They stared into each other's eyes as she contemplated the implications of his statement.

"It means," said Brandon, "that we're not safe here. The killer knows where you are."

A bewildered look covered Katie's freckled face, with the slow realization that she was still in danger. She tried to analyze the situation unemotionally, without success. Katie gazed directly into Harry's eyes, her questioning eyes beginning to well up with tears. "When's this thing gonna end? Why does he want to kill me?" she cried out.

Bobby tried to reach out and pull her close, but she jumped out of his reach, hysterically. "No! I want answers... leave me alone!"

Tina stopped making the coffee and quickly moved out of the kitchen, to go to her side. Katie hastily retreated into the living room to the bay window, where she stopped and turned to look at Brandon and Harry.

Tina approached her. "We don't know why, Katie. But I promise you that before this day's done, we'll know a lot more."

"How?"

"Trust me, we'll know a lot more about this thing, maybe even who. Funerals often have a way of reaching the truth about people, to the trained eye." She put her comforting arm around the nearly hysterical client, hugged gently and listened to Katie's troubled sobs. "Come on, let's get away from the window."

The parking lot below was quiet and filled with cars. A red Toyota, pickup truck was parked at the curb across the street. Tina's eyes caught Brandon's, with a slight nod that told him she had seen something. He stood quietly, and sauntered to the bay window. As he walked past the two women, Tina caught his arm and stopped him, while Katie walked back to Bobby Mason and sat beside him.

"There's a red Toyota, pickup parked across the street. Have a look," she whispered.

He nodded, then proceeded to the side of the window and checked out the suspect vehicle. A black and white squad car pulled up next to it, then turned left into the parking area and parked in one of the outer spaces. As the officer opened the door of his unit, the Toyota pulled away from the curb and slowly drove away.

Harrison watched, analyzing the movements of the driver over the past evening. *That Toyota isn't the same as the truck that the attacker had used when he shot out the bathroom window yesterday. Maybe it's someone else.*

Harry Garth joined him at the window. "That'll be the results from our lab boys on your friend's car. I doubt if it sheds any light on the case. There was just too much rain."

"And maybe the report on that license number. I've got a feeling it just may give us a clue to this mystery."

"We'll see. When's the funeral going to be?"

"Ten o'clock, at Pierce Brothers."

"Black and I'll be there, if at all possible." A knock on the door told them the officer was outside. Harry moved quickly to open the door. The uniformed officer stood before him with an envelope in hand. "The lab report?" Harry asked.

"Yes, sir."

"Thanks, and tell the captain that everything's quiet now, when you call in." He closed the door and opened the brown, business-size envelope. "Nothing with finger print I.D., but here's the DMV report on the license. It's registered to Michael Fallone."

"Mike?" Katie stared up at him with wide-eyed surprise at the statement. "It can't be!"

"He'll be at the funeral this morning, won't he?" Brandon asked.

"Yes! He has to come."

"Then we'll have a few questions for Mister Fallone. Harry, do me another favor, check him out again and see if he's got any other vehicles."

"You got it."

Chapter Twelve

The mortuaries around the devastated Bay area were overcrowded, as the people of the city began to bury their dead; loved ones who had fallen victim to Mother Nature's violent outburst, three days earlier. Then, there were Dan Fisher and Sarah Tulley; victims of murder. The Jastrow family of San Francisco, wealthy and influential for several decades, had made all the service arrangements for Dan Fisher.

Pierce Brothers Mortuary parking lot was filled to capacity when Tina Wolffe carefully drove her red Honda Prelude into the rear lot. Brandon sat beside her, while Katie Denton and Bobby Mason occupied the back seat, surrounded by dark green, tinted windows. Slowly, she cruised through the parking lot in search of a space. Finally, Brandon pointed at the curb directly in front of the double glass doors at the main entrance of the building. "Park right here."

"In front of the doors?" She shifted her sunglasses down onto her nose, looked at the curb, then the doors, then to Brandon. "It's a red curb."

"It's the safest place, believe me. We can get out fast to avoid any possibly dangerous situation."

"I get your drift." She drove slowly to the curb and parked.

Brandon opened the door, slid out and scanned the area through his dark sunglasses, then pulled the seat forward. Katie and Mason jumped out on his command, "Okay, it's clear. Let's get inside, quick!"

The four entered the lobby and were directed to the chapel where services were about to begin. The small, multi-denominational chapel was not overcrowded. Through the religiously decorated, stained glass windows above, a rainbow of colors reflected down onto a group of mourners in the front three sets of pews

Katie, escorted by Bobby Mason, slowly walked toward the people she knew seated in the right front row. The two PI's hung back silently, at the rear of the chapel, to observe the remorseful mourners. They sat in the last pews, quiet and inconspicuous, watching the scene unfold before the closed casket.

Aron Jastrow stood to greet Katie. He wrapped his arms around her for a few silent moments, then shook Mason's hand. A platinum blonde, about fifty years old or so, dressed in a tight, black dress, sat beside the wealthy Jastrow. She reached out with a white gloved hand, and shook Katie's hand lightly.

"My brother's wife, Patricia." the masculine voice whispered from behind Tina and Brandon. They turned around slightly, to find Richard Jastrow standing directly behind them. A strikingly beautiful woman in her mid-thirties, dressed in black, her natural blonde hair complimented by her smooth, girlish face and Irish green eyes, stood beside him. She gazed into Harrison's surprised face, then down at Tina. "Mister Harrison, Miss Wolffe... let me introduce you to my sister, Diane."

Brandon stood up and shook her hand firmly, but gently. Tina smiled from her seat in acknowledgment of her presence. "Good to meet you, Miss Jastrow," she said.

"Are you associated with our company? I don't recall ever hearing about you," Diane Jastrow inquired.

"No, just friends of Katie."

"You see, Mister Harrison and Miss Wolffe are

private investigators. They're investigating Dan's death."

"I see. You don't look like the insurance PI's we usually deal with," she quipped. Her eyes pierced his, playfully. She continued to hold his hand as if their shake was more than a greeting. "If I can help in any way at all, please, don't hesitate to call. I need to find out why Dan was murdered. We were close."

"Yes, I understand that." He stepped back, cleared his throat and put together a line of questions in his quick, analytical mind. She turned away when a low voice greeted her from behind.

"Diane. I'm so sorry." It was Michael Fallone, accompanied by a dark complexioned woman of Italian descent, her black dress reflecting the impeccable cultural influence that was her heritage.

"Oh, Mike. Why did this have to happen to poor Dan? Why?" Tears began to flow down Diane's cheeks, stinging her eyes as she tried to restrain herself from the onset of another emotional outburst. She leaned her head into his shoulder. He tenderly caressed her back in response, then wrapped his arms around the sobbing woman for a few moments.

Mike's companion watched in solemn silence, restraining her emotions as she gazed around the chapel at the other mourners, her eyes settling on Katie. Fallone released Diane Jastrow and wiped her eyes tenderly with his handkerchief. He gave her a small smile, as if to say that everything would turn out all right, then turned his attention to his companion. "Diane, you remember my friend, Gina Benado."

"Yes, how are you?" Diane remarked, her eyes still moist and her voice choked, as she tried to regain her composure.

Gina nodded silently, then whispered "I'll miss him a lot, too. I'd gotten to know him pretty well over the last couple of months." She paused, searched Mike Fallone's eyes momentarily, then looked into Brandon's remorsefully.

"So you knew him?" Diane asked curiously.

"Just through the many occasions Mike and Dan got together and I was along."

Fallone grasped Gina's arm and whispered "Let's go take our seats. We can talk later, okay?"

"Of course." Diane looked questioningly at Richard, who nodded and quietly escorted her to the first row. Mike Fallone and Gina Benado took their seats in the third row, leaving Brandon and Tina alone in the last row of pews, in quiet contemplation of the four mourners.

Next, a group of six adults and four children, all of Italian descent, entered the quiet chapel. The eldest, a strikingly handsome couple, in their late sixties, led the grieving entourage through the doors, past the two investigators. Two women and two men in their mid-thirties, dark complexioned with black hair, were followed by a twelve-year-old girl and a ten-year-old boy. A minister followed close behind, his black robes flowing elegantly as he approached, his eyes trained on a prayer book.

He looked up momentarily as he approached, catching Tina's inquisitive look. She reached out and touched the priest's arm, stopping him. "Excuse me," she whispered.

"Yes?" he replied softly.

"Who were those people who just passed?"

"The parents of Dan Fisher, his brothers and their families. You didn't know Dan, did you?"

"No, we were just acquaintances."

"It is truly a tragedy. Dan was a fine, Christian man." He turned and proceeded on to the front of the chapel as the Fisher family sat in the front, left pews. Within the next few minutes, the small chapel had filled to capacity with friends and relatives of the murdered man. Brandon and Tina watched each of the mourners enter, looking for anyone suspicious or otherwise out of place at the service.

A group of several young men and women in their mid-twenties, sat in the rear pew beside the two PI's, filling the remaining seats of the small chapel. The four men and five women chatted in whispers to each other until the service began, attracting Harrison's ear for information. "There's Katie and Bobby," said the blond man beside Harrison, "I wonder why neither of them made it to the house for the game before the quake."

"Katie should've been there before it happened," said the striking brunette woman beside him, "But she didn't get off work till five."

"Do you think she saw the murder?"

"I don't know; probably not."

Brandon looked at the man beside him, catching his attention with a quizzical stare. "Did you know Dan Fisher very well?"

"Pretty good, why?"

"Just wondering. He was Catholic, wasn't he?"

"Yes." The man nodded, answering in a whisper.

"Why aren't they having this service in a Catholic Church?"

"As I understand it, the church has been damaged by the quake."

"Hmm. Thanks." Brandon's attention was diverted to the minister, who began the religious service by quieting the congregation with a smooth wave of his hand. His low, strong voice seemed to reach out across the entire room to each individual within, including Tina and Brandon.

The service was brief, lasting approximately a half an hour. At its conclusion, everyone filed past the closed, flower covered metal casket at the front of the chapel. Harrison could detect no unusual actions from any of the congregation. Bothered by something that one of the people in the back row had mentioned, he sought out the group after they had walked by the casket and gathered toward the main doors, near the exit. Tina stayed with Katie while she spoke briefly to Dan's family near the casket.

A tall, blond, youthful man who had sat next to Harrison, idly talked to his woman companion. The woman, an attractive brunette of slender build, with a pixie-like face and dark brown eyes, peered into Brandon's eyes with deep curiosity as he approached. A smile covered her face, "Hello there! Were you a friend of Dan's?" she asked warmly.

"Not really. I never met him, but I've learned a lot about his life and death during the past couple of days." Brandon spoke in a confident manner which aroused her curiosity, as well as that of her companion and several friends. "I'm a private investigator, hired by Katie Denton to find his murderer."

"A real PI? Wow, you're certainly a cute one. Katie always had good taste, except for her choice in boyfriends."

"What'd you mean? You talking about Bobby Mason?"

"Yeah, he's a real geek. It's a personal opinion, probably held by all our friends."

"What makes him a... a geek?" Brandon stepped close to the young woman, between her and the blond man, as the group of friends surrounded him and the woman in a tight, curious circle.

"Well, mister..."

"Brandon. Brandon Harrison. And you're...?"

"Jackie. This is Steve, my boyfriend." Harrison nodded and shook his hand firmly, then stared into her brown eyes. She thought, momentarily reflecting on his question, analyzing her experiences with Bobby Mason and Katie Denton, and finally spoke out in a whisper, "I don't know. He's just not honest, you know, trustworthy."

"Yeah," agreed Steve. "He's never on time and always making excuses for himself when he's caught in a lie. He goes out on Katie a lot."

"And poor Katie, she trusts him. No matter what anyone tells her, she believes him."

"That's love, isn't it?" quipped Brandon. Jackie frowned, then looked up to see the couple they'd been talking about, approach. Katie broke away from Mason, whispering something to him as she let go of his arm. She quickly joined the group and threw her arms around Jackie. The two women hugged as tears streamed out of her sad green eyes, streaking her light make-up in flowing rivulets down her freckled cheeks. "Oh, Jackie, thanks for coming," she whimpered softly.

"Katie... oh, Katie. I can't believe this! Dan's gone, murdered! Who'd do that? Why?"

Katie pulled herself back and gazed directly into her friend's eyes. Brandon and the rest of the group watched them as she responded, "I don't know, but whoever it was thinks I saw him. He's tried to kill me a couple of times. You see, I was there."

"Oh, Katie... that's horrid! So that's why you hired this private investigator?"

"Yes. Brandon and Tina." Katie glanced

around, and saw Tina make her way into the group and stand beside Brandon, a serious look covered her solemn face and eyes. "This is Tina Wolffe and Brandon Harrison. They're kinda my bodyguards, too."

"Bobby asked me to tell you that he'd meet you later. He said that a friend was giving him a ride to pick up his car. I gave him our office phone number."

"But Bobby can't go. I need him!" Katie turned and ran away from the group, through the crowded chapel. Brandon gave Tina a nod and she swiftly followed their client to the doors, and out toward the parking lot in search of Mason.

Jackie turned to Brandon. "See what I mean? He's such a geek!"

"Yeah. Can I talk to you later about this?"

"Sure."

"I'll talk to you after the graveside service. Now I've gotta make sure Katie and Tina are okay." Brandon ran through the crowd, apprehensive about having lost sight of Katie and Tina, not to mention the unexpected actions of Bobby Mason.

Chapter Thirteen

Harrison burst through the double glass doors of Pierce Brothers Mortuary, into a crowd that had gathered on the sidewalk along the parking lot. A cool sea breeze blew in from the west, sending a chill through his thin, black, sports coat and white dress shirt. Brandon's hand moved over the deep crimson tie, under his sports coat, and released the catch on his shoulder holster for a quick draw if necessary. *A confrontation with a killer in this crowd's a definite possibility.*

Tina's shining, black hair caught his attention immediately. Katie stood beside her at the curb, next to her red Honda Prelude, scanning the parking lot and street for any sign of Bobby Mason. Brandon edged his way through the crowd of mourners along the walk, quickly reaching the two women within a couple of seconds.

"Come on, let's get back inside," he said matter-of-factly. "It's too dangerous to stand out here on the curb."

"But, Brandon..."

"No, Katie. He's gone, but he'll be back."

She turned to Tina. Tears began to trickle down her freckled cheeks, her light green eyes saddened and moist, hoping that the female member of the team would understand and let her continue the search for Bobby. "Katie, Brandon's right."

Quickly, she guided Katie back through the crowd and inside the mortuary lobby. Brandon stood at the curb for a few more moments to keep an eye on the area for a potential attack.

Then he saw a red Ford pickup parked across the street from the entrance of the parking lot. Two people occupied the truck, but at this distance he couldn't make out the face of the driver. The passenger was obscured by the driver. Brandon started toward the red truck, through a large group of people who were crossing the parking lot heading toward their cars. *Well, well! Could it be the killer?*

Suddenly, the Ford's engine roared to life. Brandon quickened his pace as the truck pulled away from the curb and slowly drove into traffic, away from the mortuary. He raced across the lot to the driveway, in an effort to glimpse the license plate, but to no avail. The truck turned right at the next street and drove out of sight.

The detective eyed Tina's Accord, then put the idea to rest. The suspect would be long gone, down one of the many hilly streets of San Francisco. "Damn," he cursed.

Upon entering the lobby, Harrison rejoined Tina and Katie, who were talking in quietly with Mike Fallone, his friend Gina, and the Jastrow brothers. Diane Jastrow quietly conversed with Dan's family in the chapel. The whole entourage would soon depart for graveside services, and a long funeral procession, through the devastated streets of the city. He had to act fast.

Tina smiled and gazed into his eyes as he approached the group. He frowned, letting her know that something was amiss. "What's up, honey?" she whispered.

He drew her aside, away from Katie and Fallone. "A red Ford pickup was parked across the street."

"Did you...?"

"No," He paused, "It drove away before I could get close. Maybe the driver saw me. I don't know."

"It might not've been the murderer, either. Well, everyone's about ready to leave for the cemetary. Should we go?"

"Yeah."

"I've gotta go to the ladies' room first."

Brandon smiled, "It's down that hall." He pointed past the chapel, at the restroom sign above a doorway.

"I'll be right back. Keep an eye on Katie." She walked away through the crowd of lingering mourners and disappeared into the restroom.

Harrison then turned to Mike Fallone, who was merely listening in on a conversation between Aron Jastrow and Katie, "So, you were Dan's partner."

"That's right," he responded. His voice reflected an irritated tone, one that warned Harrison to be careful in his questioning technique or he may scare his quarry to flight. Fallone stared at Harrison coldly, but as the private eye smiled warmly and reached to shake his hand, he unconsciously responded with a firm grasp and shake.

"Any idea on why, or who, killed him and Sarah Tulley?" Brandon's inquisitive inflection was calm and understanding of the man's feelings. Pretentious or genuine, Mike Fallone was mourning the death of a long time friend and business partner.

"Maybe." He smiled wryly for a short moment, then gazed knowingly into Brandon's inquisitive eyes, as if he knew a secret that the PI had to guess, before obtaining its revelation. "What's it to you?"

"We weren't properly introduced yesterday in the security office of the Bay Building. I'm Brandon Harrison, a private investigator. Katie hired my firm to find Dan's murderer."

Fallone stroked his thick, dark brown mustache with his fingers, contemplated Brandon's statement, then turned and walked slowly away from the group, a few feet. He leaned against the wall and motioned Harrison to join him.

"She did, huh? Well, for your information, probably any one of those people could've done it, or at least hired someone to do it." He grinned at Harrison with a brooding, suspicious look, and lit up a cigarette. "Come on outside. I don't want to offend anyone in this room. Out the side door, down here."

The two men stepped outside through a glass service entrance door at the end of the hall, onto the sidewalk, near the driveway leading to the rear parking lot. Mike Fallone nervously walked a few steps along the sidewalk, then stopped, puffed a small smoke ring from his cigarette, and leaned against the coarse exterior of the white building. He took another drag as Brandon stood a few feet away, his keen mind analyzing this nervous ex-partner.

"Let's see, you're looking for motive?"

"Among other things. What'd you mean that anyone of that group might've killed him? Was he disliked that much?"

"He had a way of sticking it to you. Gloating over minor business victories, and holding your defeats over you with antagonistic pleasure. He loved to antagonize people like Aron, Richard over there, me, and especially his two brothers. That's them... Tony and Paul." He pointed down the alley to the parking lot, where several people were getting into their cars in preparation for the short drive to the cemetery. Harrison watched them until they'd disappeared into their respective, expensive, vehicles.

"Diane Jastrow. She loved him, probably more than she should've. He treated her like a dog. I think she was getting fed up with the guy."

"Elaborate," Harrison moved a little closer to Fallone, in an effort to catch the full intent of his statement. Diane Jastrow stopped and stared at them from the front door of her white Mercedes. Her eyes greeted Harrison's, briefly. The expression on her face changed to a look of somber disapproval, then she climbed into her car.

"Diane has a mean streak. She could've done him in, in a moment of passion."

"Sarah Tulley, too?"

"It's a well known fact that Dan flirted with Sarah whenever they met. He probably used that to antagonize Diane."

"And the Jastrow brothers?"

Fallone took another long drag from his cigarette, then tossed it down onto the concrete sidewalk, crushing it out with the toe of his shoe, "The Jastrows are powerful people. Word was out that they had a shake up planned in the company. Dan was cocky and had threatened them with a million-dollar lawsuit if they got rid of him. There were shady deals in this corporate real estate office, on occasion."

"Dan threatened the Jastrows, huh?"

"Yeah. He didn't have many friends. Katie liked him, though for what reason I couldn't say."

"Now, tell me why you've been following me and Katie around." Harrison smiled at Fallone as he stepped up within arm's distance of the man, and stared intently into his, now nervous, eyes.

"I... I haven't been following you."

"You were at Katie's last night, watching her apartment. You drove right past me." Harrison stepped back to give the, now hard-breathing, nervous Fallone some thinking room. He breathed a deep sigh as the detective stared him down.

Mike lit up another Camel cigarette, took a couple of drags, and gazed up at Harrison, "I just wanted to talk to her about the murder. I was scared so I went to her place. The lights were out, so I decided to wait, out of sight. When you and

Bobby left, I saw his car was open and found the address where you had taken her. The next morning, I drove over to see her, but when the police arrived, I decided to leave. I knew I'd see her at the funeral." He gazed up at Brandon, hopeful that the detective believed his explanation. "It's the truth! I couldn't kill anyone!"

Suddenly, Tina stepped outside. Holding the glass door, she looked at Brandon, then scanned the walkway and the alley. "Is Katie with you?"

"No... she was talking to the Jastrows when I came out here with Mike."

"I can't find her!"

"Damn! Okay, check out the other parking lot. I'll ask Jastrow down here, where she is."

"Got it!" Tina disappeared inside. The door closed quietly behind her, but Harrison and Fallone didn't notice it as they ran down the alley toward Jastrow's new, black model Lincoln Continental, just backing out of its parking place.

Harrison reached the front door of the car. A startled Aron Jastrow peered out the window, then hit the window switch inside to roll it down. "What's up, Harrison?"

"Have you seen Katie? She was talking to you last."

"Yeah, she left with her friend, Bob Mason, I believe."

"That's right," echoed Richard from the passenger seat. "They're in his red MG, a '76. I believe they're heading for the cemetery. She said she'd meet us there!"

"Thanks!" He turned to Mike Fallone, who had just caught up and hadn't heard the entire conversation, "I'll see you at the cemetery later, Mike."

"No, I won't be there. I hate that kind of stuff. I'm heading home for a while, then up to the office."

"I still would like to talk to you about a few things."

"Anytime." He turned and walked away quickly, toward the red Toyota pickup parked at the other end of the lot.

Harrison turned to Aron Jastrow. He grinned at the PI, "Watch that man. He's not what he seems." With that statement, the window rolled up and Jastrow slowly drove away.

Harrison ran across the lot toward the entrance, where Tina was just coming out the door. "I can't find her!"

"She's gone with Mason!" Quickly he ran to her, standing at the curb beside the red Honda Prelude.

"Bobby?"

"Yeah. Apparently, he picked her up in a red '76 MG. Aron said they're on their way to the cemetery."

"But why wouldn't she tell you or me?" Tina opened the passenger door, then ran around to the driver's side and slid inside as Brandon got into the car.

"Well, apparently love has triumphed over intelligence," said Brandon. "They couldn't have left too long ago. Probably about the same time the Jastrows came out."

"It's my fault. I shouldn't have left her alone."

"You didn't! I did!" Brandon slipped on his dark, black-rimmed sunglasses and gazed at Tina apologetically. "See, I left her when I followed Fallone outside to hear what he had to say."

"Neither one of us thought she'd leave, though."

"Come on. Let's get to the cemetery. Our only hope is that's where they really intend to go."

Chapter Fourteen

"Katie's not here yet," said Brandon.

The dark green grass that blanketed the cemetery was short and thick, soft under the feet of the many visitors and mourners. From its beautiful tree-lined grounds, etched with colorful flower gardens and interconnected by paths leading past the resting places and stones of San Francisco's most famous historical figures, one could look over San Francisco Bay to the Golden Gate Bridge, Alcatraz Island, Angel Island and Treasure Island.

Brandon mentally noted the magnificent view as Tina stared out in awe through the heavy, wet mist at the breathtaking sight. Brandon was concerned about his client's whereabouts. Katie hadn't made it to the gravesite. Although the service wouldn't begin for several more minutes, Harrison couldn't help but feel she was in mortal danger just being with Bobby Mason. It was that little nagging voice within; the PI's intuitive, instinctual sixth sense trying to tell him to leave the funeral and find her before it was too late.

Nervously, he scanned the drive that led up the grassy hill, through the cemetery, to their graveside location, knowing she wouldn't arrive, but hoping he was wrong. Tina felt his anxiety.

Detective Harry Garth had just parked his dark blue, unmarked Chevy along the drive across from them. He and Phil Black got out and slowly started up the wet, grassy hill toward them. Harrison noted that the two police detectives were probably better dressed for the weather, in their long overcoats, than any of the rest of the mourners. They looked like police detectives, which in his estimation, was fitting for the occasion. Their mere presence could make someone in the crowd unusually nervous, and possibly reveal a clue to Fisher's murder; that is, if the killer was present.

Harrison scanned the drive once more while the two police detectives slowly approached, and then looked into Tina's worried, inquisitive eyes. She knew what he was thinking, "You don't think she's gonna get here, do you," she whispered.

"No. Bobby Mason's taken her somewhere. Either away from danger, or..." He hesitated in mid-sentence, as if it were an unspeakable thought, not to be spoken out loud and definitely not in the presence of the many mourners under suspicion. "If she doesn't arrive by the time the service begins, we're gonna split. She's not safe out there with him."

Harry Garth and Phil Black approached them. The two detectives deliberately examined each of the mourners at graveside, hoping to see a familiar face from a mug shot book. *No such luck,* Brandon thought, as the two men finally reached them.

"Well, Harrison? What've ya got for us?" Phil Black's voice was annoyingly loud, and entirely out of place, among the group of mourners. Harry punched his partner's right arm just hard enough to get his attention, then stared coldly into his eyes. Surprised, he turned to Harry with a frown.

"Take it easy, Phil," he said under his breath.

"The players are all arriving; all but Katie Denton and Bobby Mason."

"Yeah?" Harry scanned the large group gathering near the grave. A heavy mist filled the air, as though a wind had blown tiny droplets of rain from the tree leaves, down on the mourners. But there was no wind, just the fog rolling in from the bay, a short distance away. "Where are they?"

"I don't know."

"What'd you mean by that?" Phil's voice was an excited low whisper of concern. He and Harry stared at Brandon in disconcerted silence as the PI formed his answer.

Tina spoke out in their defense. "Bobby Mason escorted her away from the mortuary right after the service. They told Aron Jastrow they'd meet us here."

"They're a little late, that's all."

"Sure, Harrison." Harry observed the crowd for a moment, then examined Tina's face with an all-knowing look. "And you two don't think they're gonna show up, right?"

"You've got the general idea. We're gonna take off and try to find 'em."

"Not 'til I'm done here. I need you to introduce me to some of your prime candidates for murder." He laughed under his breath, smiling at Brandon and Tina sarcastically.

Brandon protested, "Harry, we've gotta get moving on this now. I can still find 'em while they're in the city. Once they leave..."

"What makes you think they're gonna leave?"

"I just know they're not gonna show up here and..."

"Enough. I need you here to assist us. They won't get far today. All roads leading out of the city are either closed or severely restricted with heavy traffic."

Tina looked into Brandon's angry, brown eyes, smiled and reached into her purse, pulling out her keys just above the flap, but out of the police detectives' field of vision. He knew exactly what she was contemplating, and shook his head slightly, in disagreement.

"Okay, Harrison, what's up?" Phil had seen his silent communication with Tina, but hadn't caught the whole meaning of his actions.

"Yeah. And where's Mike Fallone?" asked Harry.

"Fallone didn't come to the funeral here, but he was at the mortuary," said Brandon. Glad to change the subject, he pointed out Fallone's girlfriend in the crowd beside Aron and Richard Jastrow. Diane stood beside Richard. "That's his girlfriend, Gina Benado, standing next to Aron Jastrow. She was at the service with him, but he told me he was going to the office. He can't stand funerals."

"What else did he say?"

"Only that he wanted to make sure that Katie was all right. That's why he drove to her place last night, and was out in front of Tina's this morning. He said he didn't know who had done it, but it could've been any number of these people present."

"He did, did he?" Phil gazed around at the mourners, smiled, and shook his head at Brandon.

Harry started toward Gina, motioning for the PI to follow, "Come on. I need an introduction to Miss Benado."

"Right." Harrison and Tina followed him around the gathering crowd, past Jackie and her group of friends. Tina hesitated beside them, "I don't like it, Tina." warned Brandon.

"Just let me disappear in the crowd. I'll drive over to Katie's apartment and have a look. If they're not there, I'll come right back." She stared confidently into his concerned eyes and smiled, "Harry'll never know I've gone. Besides, he wants you, not me."

"Okay. But come back right away if they aren't there. If you don't return by the time this thing is over, I'm coming to get you, so stay put."

"You got it. I'll keep them there at gunpoint."

Garth turned to make sure they were following and motioned to them to hurry. Brandon smiled and picked up his pace. "Get going, honey, and be careful. Don't take any chances."

"You can count on it." Tina stopped, then blended unobtrusively into the group beside Jackie. After watching Brandon approach Gina with Garth and Black, she turned and quickly made her way down the wet, grassy hillside to the drive where her red Honda Prelude was parked. She opened the door, slid inside and started the engine.

Harrison caught a glimpse of her driving down the drive, as Harry faced Gina Benado and said, "Excuse me, Miss Benado? I'm detective Garth, San Francisco Police Department."

She turned, startled by his introduction. "Yes?" Then she recognized Brandon standing beside him, and smiled fleetingly.

"Brandon Harrison here said you might be able to give me some information on Mike Fallone."

Gina stared at him momentarily, with her dark Italian eyes, questioning the police detective with a discerning look of defiance. "What do you want of Mike?" Her response was whispered defiantly as she glared at him spitefully.

"I just have a few questions for him."

"I don't know where he is, and even if I did, I wouldn't tell you." Gina folded her arms and stared intently at the grave.

Aron turned to Brandon and the two police detectives with an irritated glare. "Do you have to annoy people just before the service? Why don't you wait until it's over? There'll be plenty of time to investigate these murders then."

"Sorry, Mr Jastrow," replied Harry. "I just have a couple questions."

"Harry, not now," said Harrison, calmly. "Let's wait, as requested."

Garth grunted his disapproval, then stood back behind Gina, with Phil Black and Brandon on either side of him. He gazed into Brandon's smiling eyes and grinned with a wink. They both turned to look at Black, who held an angry frown across his face. "Phil takes this stuff too seriously," whispered Harry.

"And you don't?"

"It's all an act. We all must put on our best performances during moments like these. By the way, that was a nice performance that Tina put on, slipping away almost unnoticed."

"Yes, she's great, isn't she?"

"Humph. Where's she going? In search of Miss Denton?"

"Nice guess. You just said you needed me to introduce you to Gina... not Tina. So, we decided it would be best if she followed the trail before it got cold."

Garth smiled his disapproval with a raised right eyebrow. "As long as you're here, that's all I need. I hope she doesn't get into trouble, that's all."

"Tina's a big girl. I've trained her well. I doubt if she'll need my assistance, and if she does, I'll know."

"Yeah? How?"

"I'll just know. We have a thing between us... a mind link, if you will."

"Sure, Harrison." Harry laughed quietly, his eyes gleaming and a grin on his face. Black turned to see what his partner was chuckling about, retaining the angry frown on his face.

"Say, Harry, doesn't Phil ever smile?"

"He's a serious kind of fellow, especially in times such as these... and places like this."

Harrison nodded, then gazed around at the

participants in the graveside service. The priest began with a prayer. Harrison hoped the service would be short, but knowing the Catholic Church, knew it would probably be much longer than he liked.

The Earth trembled under the mourners for a few anxious moments, and the priest went silent. Then the murmur of voices rose from the large group. The priest quieted them with a wave of his hand and continued.

Brandon looked out across the cemetery in hopes that Tina's red Honda would appear on the drive. Somehow, he knew it wouldn't. All he could do for her now was to pray that she could find Katie and Bobby and persuade them to return with her. He hoped that she didn't encounter the killer along the way.

Chapter Fifteen

Katie Denton stood before her living room window in uncertain silence, wishing there were a way to call Tina or Brandon to let them know that she was all right, and to reassure them that she and Bobby Mason knew what they were doing by taking flight from the dangerous, life-threatening situation that she was constantly facing. She peered down from her second floor to see Bobby park the little red MG at the back of the parking lot, then climb into his white Toyota Celica.

In a few moments, he would have it parked in front of the stairs. I'll have to hurry and pack everything I'll need for a couple of weeks' vacation in the north. This city gives me the creeps. A killer out there! Earthquakes! Funerals! Why didn't I leave before this?

She hurried into her bedroom and opened the large sliding closet door to reveal her wardrobe hanging orderly within. Then she began to hastily select the clothes she would take, laying them out neatly on the California king size bed to be packed in one large suitcase.

The front door in the living room slammed shut. "Katie!" Bobby called out anxiously, his voice irritated and demanding. "Are you packed yet?"

"Almost! Come in and help me."

He hurried into her bedroom, then stopped and watched her as she pulled out a couple of colorful ski sweaters. She turned to him, holding both sweaters up for his approval. "What'd' ya think? This one... or this one?"

"I don't know, they're both nice. Bring 'em both... but hurry. We've gotta get out of here fast. We don't need to be discovered by Brandon and Tina, or the police, or..."

"Don't say it!" she snapped. "I'm almost ready."

Katie quickly finished placing her clothing into the large suitcase, closed it and picked it up as if to test its weight. "Just right! Here, take it down to the car while I get my makeup bag and a few bathing things."

"Okay... just hurry!"

"A couple minutes... I'll be right down."

He frowned, picked up the luggage, and stomped out of the room. Irritated, Katie gazed at herself in the mirror. Her sad, freckled girlish face looked tired and frightened at what was transpiring, and of the events of the last couple of days. Am I going crazy? Should I go? Gotta call Tina.

Katie grabbed her purse from the bed, dug through it, and found a small piece of paper with Harrison-Wolffe Investigation's phone number scrawled on it in detective Garth's handwriting. She picked up the bedside phone and quickly punched in the number.

Harrison's voice answered on the message tape. At the beep, she said, "Tina! Brandon! This is Katie. I'm okay. I'm with Bobby. We're going away together. Thanks for all your help. I'll send you a check for your services after we reach Por... our destination. I'm not exactly sure where it is or when we'll get there." She paused, thought, then continued, on the verge of tears. "Thanks, again. Sorry I almost got you killed. Bye."

Slowly and thoughtfully, she put the phone in its cradle, hesitating in case there was something she forgot to say. Her make-up bag had been already packed, but she opened it and checked through the contents just to make sure she hadn't forgotten anything vital.

Satisfied, she closed it and grabbed her purse. After stuffing the Harrison-Wolffe Investigation phone number into her wallet, she checked to see that her ATM card was still there, picked up the make-up bag, slung her purse over her right shoulder, glanced around the room and left her apartment, locking it behind her.

Mason watched her walk slowly and thoughtfully toward the stairs which led down to him and his car, parked at the foot of the stairway. "It's about time, Katie! Come on, let's go!" He pleaded while he held the car door wide open.

Suddenly, the earth trembled beneath their feet, then began to shake violently for a few tension filled moments. Katie held on to the railing of the staircase, a frightened, questioning look in her terrified eyes. Bobby quietly ran up the stairs two at a time to her aid.

He reached her side more than three quarters of the way up, just as the minor trembler stopped and the swaying stairs stabilized beneath them. "Oh Bobby, that was scary. Get me out of this town, far away... okay?" Tears of fright filled her green eyes that gazed into his.

"That's what I'm trying to do. Now, come on." He held her arm and helped Katie down the stairs and into the car. She smiled with uncertainty, looked back up at her apartment, then strapped on her seat belt. Bobby Mason started the car and drove out of the parking lot, turning north on Sunset toward Golden Gate Park and the majestic bridge.

Katie stared out the windshield at the nearly deserted street. Usually at that time in the early afternoon those same streets were crowded with a continuous flow of heavy traffic, especially so on Friday. Bobby turned right, up Judah, and drove cautiously at a moderate speed toward Highway One North, not wanting to draw attention to them by breaking any speed laws.

He made a left onto Highway One, 19th Street, the thoroughfare through Golden Gate Park, past Strawberry Hill and Stow Lake, deserted with the exception of a car or two driving south bound. As they exited the park and 19th Street changed to Park Presidio Boulevard, Bobby noticed the red pickup truck following about a block behind with two other cars.

He adjusted the rearview mirror for a better look. "Didn't Harrison say that the killer used a red pickup truck?"

"Yeah." She looked at him, startled by the question. As he looked in the mirror, Katie turned to peer out the rear window. A chill ran uncontrolled down her back when she caught sight of the red pickup behind them, about a quarter of a mile away. She stared for almost thirty seconds, trying to determine the make of the ominous truck. "It's a Toyota," she said.

"I think it's been following us for a couple of miles."

"It's not the killer," she said confidently. "Brandon said that the killer had a red Ford truck." They stared out ahead with a deep sigh of relief. Bobby Mason accelerated, picked up speed to fifty and entered the tunnel at the Presidio, extending their lead over the red Toyota.

"All the same, we'd better put some distance between us. I wanna get away from this city fast."

"Yeah. I hope an aftershock doesn't hit while we're in this tunnel. It seems to have held up okay." She looked through the side window at the rapidly passing tunnel wall, breathing shallowly and almost imperceptibly in fear that the tunnel might collapse and bury them forever.

He increased speed to sixty as they exited on the approach to the Golden Gate Bridge, a mile ahead, keeping his eye on the rear view mirror. Traffic increased as they neared the entrance, slowing them to nearly thirty miles an hour. Katie turned around and peered out the back window. "It's gone!"

"Good! Guess you were right, it wasn't the killer." Within a few moments, they drove onto the magnificent but fog enshrouded Golden Gate Bridge and began their drive over the cold bay, far below. Traffic was still slower than he'd have liked, but began to pick up speed at about the halfway point.

"Please, God... no earthquakes now," Katie whispered. They gazed nervously into each other's eyes momentarily, then out at the misty road toward the end of the bridge. Turning her eyes to the bay, she saw Alcatraz in the distance, then it too disappeared into a foggy mist. *I wonder how that old prison held up? Probably not a bit of damage. Maybe we should hide out there. No, Bobby's right. We gotta get out of the city... north to Eureka or even better, Portland.*

A short distance north of the Golden Gate Bridge they sped past Alexander exit, the road to one of Katie's favorite towns around the bay, Sausalito. She wondered how the town had fared during the last couple days since the "big one" on Tuesday, with its stair stepped hill houses Precariously rising above the town. Sausalito could easily appear to be a Southern European seacoast village, its harbors full of small vessels of varied sizes and shapes and its shops and restaurants concentrated at the water's edge. She had spent many a Saturday afternoon shopping along Bridgeway in The Village Fair with its forty small specialty shops of intriguing handcrafted imports from all over the world.

Katie anxiously tried to get a glimpse of the town as they drove over the hill on 101. She gazed down at Sausalito as they sped by it at close to seventy-five miles an hour. There were no boats on Richardson Bay. The town looked quiet and peaceful, but then it always seemed that way from a distance. "I wish we could go down to Sausalito, Bobby. I hope it's okay, not too much damage. That seven point could've really destroyed it."

"Yeah. Maybe when this is all over," he said sternly. "Right now, we are heading for Santa Rosa."

"Santa Rosa? Why there?"

"Because my brother lives there. We can get some supplies for the trip; sandwich things and drinks. We'll only stay long enough to get what we need." Bobby rolled down the window all the way and waved his arm out through the opening. He smiled at her warmly, took out a cigarette from his shirt pocket, punched in the lighter in the dash, then put the white rolled tobacco between his lips.

The lighter popped out. Katie reached down and pulled it out with her finger tips, then brought the small hot tip to the end of his cigarette. He breathed in and the cigarette was lit. She didn't like smoking, but somehow put up with Bobby's. He'd promised to quit on several occasions, but every time he tried, some stressful situation would deter him and he'd be back to his old habit once again.

She decided not to press it on this occasion. She didn't want to irritate him under these circumstances. As Sausalito and Richardson Bay passed from view, Katie turned her thoughts to the murderer, and the possible reasons why he would've killed Sarah and Dan.

And why would he want to kill her? There hadn't been much time to contemplate the events of the murders. She wondered if Bobby had, but reluctant to ask, kept it to herself.

I didn't see the guy. Was there something I missed? I can't remember anything except those hands that picked me up from the floor... then sent me hurtling into the black opening. And the horrible Earthquake... that horrible rumbling and crashing. But there's no face to remember. It must be something I knew about Dan and Sarah. But what? Dan never said anything about her except that she was cute. He couldn't have been having an affair with her!

Katie turned to Bobby, who was concentrating on the road and taking a drag on his cigarette. "Do you think Dan and Sarah were having an affair?"

He glanced at her momentarily, then took another quick drag. "I guess it's a possibility. If they were, Diane Jastrow probably wouldn't like it very much."

"But Diane wouldn't kill them... and me. Besides, it was a man that tried to kill me."

"She could've hired it done. She's wealthy." With a quick glance, he changed lanes to the left and passed two slower vehicles, tossing the more than half-smoked cigarette out the window. "Don't even think about it, sweetheart. Let the police figure it out. Maybe Harrison'll find out."

"Brandon and Tina will. I just have a feeling that there's something I know about, but I can't remember."

He took a hold of her hand tenderly and gazed into her worried green eyes, a warm smile on his lips. "Try not to think about it."

Katie slid over close to him and rested her head against his shoulder. "You're right. It'll come to me if I don't think about it. That's the way it always works."

Chapter Sixteen

Tina Wolfe turned her red Honda Prelude right off Sunset into the apartment parking lot. After stopping momentarily for a quick scan of the complex, she drove slowly through the nearly empty lot toward the north end parking area next to Katie's building. Then she spotted it, parked a few spaces away in front of the building, to the right of Katie's apartment.

A red MG. It's gotta be Mason's. Guess I'd better go out up there. If they're here, I have to try to surprise them.

She reached into the glove compartment and retrieved her 9 mm Beretta and carefully slipped the loaded weapon into her handbag.

Okay, Ginger, I may need you... but I hope not.

Opening the car door, she cautiously stepped out into the chilled early afternoon air. A wind blew gently over her shapely legs. Tina slipped her sunglasses over her eyes, then began to walk toward what she presumed was Katie's apartment. According to Brandon, it was the first unit on the left, at the top of the stairs.

Quickly, she walked across the parking lot. Her thin black skirt and white blouse covered only by a black, lightweight jacket, an outfit she rarely wore because she hadn't attended many funerals, wasn't exactly appropriate for the cool breeze that blew right through it to her skin. She wanted to run up the stairs and get inside out of the cold, but instinct warned to be extra cautious.

As she approached the stairs, her hand reached slowly into her black leather purse, grasped 'Ginger', then slowly removed the handgun. She slipped it under her jacket, out of sight, but ready for use.

Tina glanced around the parking lot with a discerning eye. It appeared to be empty of any suspicious people... or anyone, for that matter. Her eyes turned to the quiet apartment at the top of the stairs, the door to which was located several feet to the right, opposite the three foot high wrought-iron railing.

Taking two steps at a time, she ran crouched up the stairs. Reaching the top, she stopped on the second to last stair, pulled Ginger from under her jacket, released the safety, then held it to her side and cautiously proceeded to the door.

It was quiet inside; no sounds of life at all emanated from within.

She pressed her ear to the door and listened, but still nothing. The doorknob wouldn't turn. It was locked, as she suspected it would be. She knocked lightly, twice. Still silence.

No one home, I guess.

She knocked a little louder, waited for a second, then pulled out her favorite lock pick, inserted it, and worked the lock. In seconds she felt the tumbler lined up and she turned the handle, opening the door slightly.

She peered inside. A cramped kitchen in the far corner opened to the small dinette with a circular table and four white matching swivel chairs. After listening for the slightest sound, she entered closing the door behind her and locking it. The living area spread out before her, approximately twenty feet long and maybe twelve feet wide, filled sparsely with a light mauve pillowed sofa along the wall and a matching love seat that faced her in front of the sliding glass door, which was covered by mauve drapes. An entertainment center with stereo unit, television, glassed-in bookcase containing small crystalline figures and other mementos of her life faced the sofa.

The only bedroom, the door to which was located beside the entertainment center, was dark, its blinds pulled tightly together so that no prying eyes could see into the window at the far end. She flicked on the light switch inside the door. The bedroom, lit up by a bedside light, revealed a king size bed, a mirrored oak dresser, an open closet with a lot of space between the hangers, and a large bathroom.

Hmm. Her closet's too empty.

Tina walked into the bathroom and checked her countertop, sink, and medicine cabinet. She opened the drawers, then finally checked the shower bath tub.

Almost all her makeup and other things are gone... no shampoo, no hair dryer no... where'd you go, Katie?

After a thorough search of the room, dresser drawers, the closet and night stand, she moved to the living room. An intense search told her nothing of where her client had gone. Tina walked over to the sliding glass door, pulled the drapes open slightly, then peered outside.

Unable to see the parking lot past the half wall that bordered the small patio area, she slid open the door and walked out onto the patio. Bobby Mason's red MG was still parked down there in front of the next building. Maybe... that's it! They're in his other car, the one he left last night.

Her eyes darted around the parking lot in search of an unknown vehicle. What kind of car does he have? Call Brandon on his car phone. She picked up the cordless receiver and punched in his car phone number then remembered he doesn't have his car. Hmm... Harry! I can get Harry through the Police department.

Tina stared down at the parking lot as her mind brought up the often used number of Harry Garth's desk. "Homicide, McCarthy." The voice was that of Pam McCarthy, the twenty-nine year old blonde officer who appeared to be too feminine to be on the force but knew exactly what she was doing when it came to police investigations.

"Hi, Pam, this is Tina Wolffe."

"Tina, what's up?"

Tina's voice carried a professional, concerned tone as she continued. "I need to get a hold of Brandon. He's with Harry at the cemetery. Can you patch me through?" She paused and waited for Pam McCarthy's response.

"Well... I really shouldn't..."

"Please, Pam. I'll owe ya one."

"Just a second. I hope Harry doesn't get mad. Oh, what the hell. Just hold on, okay?"

"Pam, wait. Just have Harry tell Brandon to call me at this number. Tell him to hurry, okay?"

"You got it, Tina."

She gave Pam the number and hung up, then walked back out onto the patio. A small, glass-topped, black wrought-iron table and two matching chairs occupied the far end of the deck. She casually walked toward them, still eyeing the parking lot below, then sat down in the closest chair.

It occurred to her that while she had a phone in her hand she should check their answering machine for any messages. Her fingers quickly punched in their home office phone number. It rang four times, then Brandon's voice came on, telling the caller to leave a message. She punched in her access code.

After two hang-ups, Katie's voice spoke out

into the receiver. The message was apologetic, then she caught it. "Por!" She listened to the rest of the message. "Sure, Katie! You're going to Portland? With Bobby Mason? Come on, Brandon. Call, please!"

She hung up the phone by moving the off switch and resetting it to "Ready". Then Tina got up from her seat and started inside, still watching the parking lot.

Suddenly, her eyes caught sight of a dark red pickup truck pulling into the parking lot at the far end. She watched it approach slowly past the apartment buildings.

It's a Ford. I wonder.

The truck parked near the red MG, two spaces on the other side of it.

Tina sat back down on the chair, constantly observing the truck, hoping to make out the driver when he got out. Several long seconds passed, but the driver didn't make a move. She trained her eyes on the truck, keeping low so the occupant couldn't see her.

The phone rang in her hand. Startled, she hit the answer switch, hoping that whoever it was in the red Ford pickup didn't hear it too. "Hello?" she answered.

"Tina! What've you got?"

"Trouble, Brandon," she whispered. "I'm at Katie's. She's gone, but the red Ford pickup just arrived. It just parked there!"

"Can you see anyone inside?"

"I can't I.D. him, but he's there." She peered out over the concrete half wall at the truck. Then, she realized what was going on. "Brandon! He's gone!"

"You mean the truck's gone?"

"No! The driver's gone!"

"Get out now!" he screamed.

Suddenly, the sliding glass door shattered in a series of loud explosions. A bullet impacted loudly into the wall behind her head. Tina dove for the floor and crawled to the corner under the table, phone in hand. "What the... Brandon! I'm under fire!"

"Shit! You got your gun?"

"Yeah!" She grabbed Ginger from out of her purse beside her. "Got it."

"I'm on my way. Harry, get some cars over to Katie's. Tina's under attack."

She heard his voice in the background, excited and distant. "Right! Tell her we're on our way."

"Keep down, Tina. I'll be there in a couple minutes."

Tina heard the phone hang up, then another bullet slammed into the wall above her.

Where are you? Better not look. Gotta get inside while you're still down there.

Flattened down on the floor, she scurried over the broken glass and into the apartment through the totally shattered glass door. Blood dripped from the palm of her left hand and the tips of her ring and middle fingers. She sat against the wall behind the love seat and painfully picked out the glass fragments.

Then, without further hesitation, she ran to the door, opened it and peered outside. "Where are you? Why are you shooting at me? Do you think I'm Katie?"

He's on the other side. I don't think he's out there at the bottom of the stairs yet.

She quickly peered in the other direction, past the other two apartments to a balcony overlooking the next apartment complex. A six foot concrete wall reached up almost to the balcony, bordered on top by a black wrought-iron railing .

That's it. My only escape.

Without a moment's hesitation, she ran out the door. Closing it quietly, she ran in a crouched position, gun in hand, for the wrought-iron fence.

Suddenly, the glass window shattered above her in a hail of glass. A woman's hysterical scream echoed from the apartment. She dove frantically to the ground for cover, flattening herself on it. An icy chill ran through her body as she aimed her black Beretta at the stairway leading up from the parking lot, her finger tensing on the trigger, ready to squeeze off several rounds into her attacker.

The apartment door opened next to the bullet smashed the window. A frightened girlish face peered out, her brunette hair up in curlers. "Get back inside! NOW!"

The sight of the black gun in her hand sent the woman back inside, slamming the door loudly.

Her eyes returned to the stairs. Someone was slowly crawling up them. A man wearing a brown leather flight jacket, his face obscured by a stocking mask, appeared with gun in hand pointed in her direction.

He stared menacingly at Tina on the ground, then aimed at her with a large black automatic handgun.

Her gun exploded with two loud shots that echoed through the corridors of the complex. The man whirled around, stumbled, and dashed down the stairs.

Cautiously, Tina got up in a crouch and moved to the apartment's shattered window. Then the truck moved to life, its wheels spinning, burning rubber on the asphalt.

Tina stood up and ran to the stairs. The red

Ford turned sharply, ready to speed out of the lot. She aimed at the cab where the driver's head should've been. Before she got a shot off, he had stuck his gun out the window and fired. Two bullets slammed into the stairs below her and ricocheted into the wall.

She squeezed the trigger. 'Ginger' exploded violently as it fired a nine millimeter slug into the rear window of the pickup, shattering it into millions of pieces.

The truck swerved, turned and straightened out, sped to the exit and disappeared out of the lot. Tina ran down the stairs, across the parking lot to her car and opened the door. "My keys!" She realized her keys were in her purse on the patio. "Damn it!"

She turned and walked slowly back to the stairs. As she started up, a black and white police car roared into the lot, its lights flashing on top. Then, an unmarked dark blue car drove in, a small red light whirling over the driver's door. She recognized the passenger at once.

"Brandon, thank God!" She sighed.

As the black and white pulled up, followed by Garth's car, she caught sight of the red crimson trail of blood snaking ominously along the wet sidewalk and pooling in puddles of dirty water.

"I got him!"

Chapter Seventeen

Harry stood before the shattered splintered sliding patio door of Katie's apartment, contemplating the dynamics of the latest attack on Tina Wolffe. The lab team, having arrived barely fifteen minutes after he called them, were in the process of carefully digging out the remains of the bullets lodged in the outside wall of the apartment.

"They almost killed me! My window! That woman had a gun!" The hysterical voice of the young woman next door permeated the apartment. The calm voice of one of San Francisco's finest tried to reassure her that it was over. Her crying and hysteria prompted Harrison to get up from the sofa, where he'd been tending to Tina's hand. After finding a bottle of Bactine in the medicine cabinet, he carefully picked out the glass splinters embedded in her palm, applied the medication, then carefully wrapped her hand in gauze, all the while listening to the hysterical neighbor. He and Tina needed quiet to figure out the whys and wherefores of her near deadly encounter with Fisher and Sarah's murderer.

"Dollars to donuts that those slugs are identical to the ones..."

"You're probably correct in your assessment, Harrison." Harry Garth turned to the pair of PI's as Brandon gently closed the front door, which effectively eliminated the neighbor's annoying tantrum. "But why? Why this attack on you, Tina?"

"He probably thought I was Katie, don't you think? That's all I can come up with."

Harry frowned, paced across the living room and peered into the bedroom, then turned to her. "Maybe it's someone who wants to kill you. Did you ever think about that?"

"No! Well, not really." She gazed up at Brandon with confused, questioning eyes. He dismissed the notion with a wave of his hand and grinned at Harry.

"I know what you're getting at. She's a private investigator. So am I. I'd be the more likely candidate to be shot at, to be killed. No, she hasn't been in the business long enough to make an enemy like that."

"Just bringing up the obvious," Garth retorted.

"Yeah, well, forget it. It was a case of mistaken identity. Katie was supposed to be here, not Tina." He gave a disconcerting frown to Garth, then gazed into Tina's dark brown wondering eyes and sat down beside her on the sofa.

"Maybe Harry's right," she whispered. "Look at the facts. First, Katie's nearly killed when the murderer pushed her into the elevator shaft."

"Okay. Then she comes to our place yesterday," Brandon continued. "She was almost killed in that hail of bullets that ripped apart our bathroom."

"Our bathroom, Brandon. Those bullets could've been meant for me... it's my house."

"Or for me," he countered.

"Then, we're in the Bay Building. I accompanied her to the women's room and the murderer made another attempt on Katie's life... or was it mine? Each time since the original attempt on Katie was made, I've been there! Even in the garage, when the murderer was trying to get away."

"Okay, so you were there," he retorted in frustration. "So was Katie Denton, and no one was shooting at you or had a reason to kill you before Katie knocked on our door."

"Well, no one was trying to kill Katie before Tuesday, either. I'm not convinced that this isn't coincidence. Maybe I'm the target."

Harry Garth strolled back to the broken window. Outside, his lab team was working. "We should find out soon enough, soon as we get a slug out of the wall."

"Got a good one, Harry." A tall, six foot two blond lab man stood up on the patio. His friendly blue eyes laughed as he smiled and approached Garth, holding in his palm a small gnarled and crushed metal object. He stepped through the broken window and handed the crushed slug to Harry. "Twenty-two caliber, I'd say."

"Yeah, you're right. Pull the others too, then get the ones in front."

"You got it."

"Anyone working on the blood samples?"

"Yeah. We'll have it analyzed in about an hour. You'll have a full report by late this afternoon on the ballistics and blood."

"Right! Well, Harrison, Tina? Twenty-two, and I'll bet they're just like those found in your bathroom and in the Bay Building. Either our man's using two different guns, or we've got two different people."

"Or maybe a conspiracy?" Brandon stood up and looked at the twisted slug in his friend's hand. Harry handed it to him for inspection. "There's gotta be a tie-in."

"What about Katie?"

Tina jumped up from the sofa and stood beside her man. "She's traveling north with Mason. Portland, I think. She stopped midword, realizing what she was about to say, so I'm not sure if it's Portland or some other place."

Brandon thought momentarily, paced to the window and glanced outside. Analyzing the facts just presented to his analytical and quick- thinking mind, he desperately sought the missing piece to the puzzle, a piece that would head his investigation in the right direction. What had he overlooked?

"I wonder how badly you wounded your attacker?"

"I don't know, but he was able to drive and shoot at the same time."

Harry approached Brandon, followed closely by Tina. "We've notified all the hospitals to be on the alert for gunshot wounds. The department has an APB out on the red Ford pickup. We'll find him."

"And we have to find Katie." Tina stared up into her man's thoughtful eyes as he turned to see a questioning look of genuine concern cross her face.

"Tina's right." Harrison nodded to her, then threw a quick smiling glance at Harry. "We're out of here! We'll let you know what we find out."

"Harrison, you can't take her now. She's a prime witness here to a shooting attempt. I've got a lot more questions, and I'm sure the captain will too."

"She's coming with me. I won't let Tina out of my sight again; not while we've got this creep running around free out there."

"Damn, Harrison! Okay, but keep in touch. If I get anything, I'll call on your car phone."

"We'll be in Tina's car. Here's her number." Brandon pulled out his wallet from the breast pocket of his black tweed wool suit coat and palmed his business card from it. "Here, it's the third number down. Let's go, honey. We've got some long miles to go to catch Katie and Bobby."

Harry Garth watched his two friends rush out the door. He stepped outside as if to follow, but hesitated and watched their hasty descent down the stairs. They ran across the parking lot and got into Tina's red Accord. Brandon slid into the driver's seat while Tina rode shotgun.

"Good luck," he mumbled to himself.

Brandon gave a salute-like wave as they drove past the building. "Okay, Tina, what's the quickest way to the Golden Gate from here?"

"Sunset to Lincoln to Nineteenth."

Suddenly, a red Toyota, pickup truck which neither Brandon nor Tina had seen coming up Sunset toward them in the right lane skidded to a screeching halt, inches away from the front of the Prelude's as yet unscratched black bumper.

Harrison realized who it was immediately. Sticking his head out through the already opened window beside him, he yelled, "Fallone! What the hell're you doing?"

"Is Katie all right?" He shouted over the loud engine noise of his truck.

"I don't know."

"I heard on the police band on my CB that there were gun shots at this address... Katie's apartment!

"Katie wasn't here. Someone fired at Tina."

"Did she get him?"

"No, and he got away before the police could arrive. She may have wounded him."

"Good. I'm glad Katie... and Tina are all right."

"Now, if you'll move out of the way, we gotta go."

"Right."

The red Toyota pulled ahead to the curb, out of the path of their Prelude. Brandon drove out, left onto Sunset, and picked up speed toward Lincoln. He kept the red Toyota pickup in sight in his rearview mirror, watching it parked at the curb. Its driver, Fallone, remained inside.

"Do you think he's telling the truth?" Tina asked. She leaned back in the soft bucket seat and gazed questioningly at her man. Brandon continued driving on up Lincoln in silence, analyzing the short confrontation with Fallone only scant moments before.

"I don't know. Maybe."

"Are we going north to find Katie?"

"No, not yet. I want to check out the funeral reception at Aron Jastrow's estate. There are still a lot of questions I need to ask of some of the people he's invited up for the afternoon."

"So you don't think that Katie's in danger?"

"Katie and Bobby are escaping the city and all its dangers. I think he's honestly trying to help her." He smiled and looked into Tina's curious sparkling brown eyes, knowing that her concern for their client's welfare and safety was paramount. "Knowledge of their whereabouts is unknown to us and probably everyone else involved, including the murderer. Mike Fallone's concern for Katie's welfare worries me. I wonder why he came to Katie's apartment. I wonder how he knew we'd be there."

"Brandon, let's not jump to conclusions without supporting evidence. We'll find out soon enough."

"Right you are, my dear." He turned left onto Nineteenth Street, which would take them through Golden Gate Park to the bridge. "We should be able to figure out his motives at the Jastrow residence. I've got a feeling he'll be there, too."

"Where does Aron Jastrow live?"

"Tiburon, across the bay."

"I should've known." She smiled with the knowledge that many of the wealthy population of the City by the Bay made their homes, estates of the good life, along the eastern shore of

Richardson Bay in Belvedere and Tiburon in Marin County, just across the Golden Gate Bridge. "Maybe Katie's going to Jastrows'! There's no reason for her to go north, as we think. Why would she want to go so far away?"

"I can think of one good reason—escape."

"But it's a possibility she'll turn up at the reception, don't you think?"

"It's possible, but highly unlikely. You see, she wants to escape death, not walk into its open arms."

Brandon accelerated the red Honda into the tunnel at Presidio. Tina sighed with relief that the power had been restored to the lights on the curved ceiling and along the walls. Within moments they exited, much to her relief, and merged with the 101 traffic heading north across the Golden Gate Bridge.

A low fog had rolled in across the bay, which gave an eerie appearance to the great bridge. Its tall towers peeked through the upper layer of gray fog, while the main highway level was engulfed in the thick, wet cloud of dense mist.

Harrison hoped that the reception at Jastrow's Tiburon home would lift the shroud of fog that covered the true circumstances and motives concerning the murders of Dan Fisher and Sarah Tulley.

Hopefully all of the suspects would be there in one place, with the exception of Bobby Mason. And he might even show up. If so, Katie's life would be in certain danger.

Chapter Eighteen

"What a beautiful view, Brandon!" Tina gazed out at the Jastrow estate perched on a hilltop overlooking Richardson Bay, directly opposite Sausalito, one of several huge estates of the affluent that covered the hills of Tiburon and Belvedere. The gated Jastrow home, ensconced on ten hillside acres, appeared safe and sheltered in a grove of large Douglas Fir, tan oak, alder, buckeye and California laurel.

The home, recently constructed by Aron at the request of his wife, replaced the sixty year old twenty-six room mansion they had originally purchased ten years earlier. Pattie could not satisfy her need to keep warm in the old building, even though efforts to insulate it sufficiently were made on two occasions. The cold breezes penetrated the old house that sat vulnerable to the harsh winds that blow across the bay. Now it sat vacant, situated on the bluffs above.

She and Aron designed their new five level, sixty-two hundred square foot home complete with gymnasium, tennis courts and Olympic size pool to entertain her friends. Aron usually felt that there wasn't enough time in the day for work, let alone entertaining friends, so he left that job to Pattie, who alone decorated their new, modern custom-designed mansion.

Brandon Harrison drove Tina's Prelude slower than most of the light traffic along Tiburon Boulevard. She gazed out the open window at Sausalito, nestled in the hills on the other side of the bay. She had only visited the small town on one occasion after arriving in the Bay area almost a year earlier, and had never been to Tiburon or Belvedere.

They approached the Jastrow Estate only after driving up several winding roads, which without the precise directions that Aron Jastrow had provided Brandon at the cemetery, would have been almost impossible to locate. As they reached their destination at the end of a narrow road, the view overlooking Richardson Bay was magnificent. Tina hadn't quite expected the beautiful breathtaking dramatic scene of the San Francisco Bay that unfolded before her awe-filled eyes.

She stared out quietly at the city lying still and apparently unscathed across the bay. Brandon stopped the car at the side of the narrow road. The two stepped outside and stood at the edge of the road, high above Tiburon and Belvedere, to take in the full scope of the panoramic scene from Richardson Bay and Sausalito to the Golden Gate Bridge, the city, and to the east, the quake-damaged Oakland Bay Bridge.

"Oh Brandon! This is so beautiful. I never imagined such a sight like this existed!" Tina's voice reflected her awe at the splendor of the view before them. "Wouldn't it be nice to wake every morning to that?"

Brandon wrapped his arm around her small waist and gazed into her beaming eyes, smiling in his warm, affectionate way. "Yeah. You like this view, too? It's nice all right."

The serenity of their moment, alone, overlooking the bay, was suddenly interrupted with the squealing sound of tires of an approaching car traveling much too fast for that remote winding road. They both turned to see Aron Jastrow's black Continental appear as it rounded a sharp turn from around the hill and picked up speed as it approached them.

Aron Jastrow abruptly pulled the Lincoln up

next to them. The dark green tinted front passenger window slid down with the faint hum of its electric motor, and Richard Jastrow poked his head through the open window and smiled at the two PI's. "Glad to see you made it. Follow us through the security gate", he shouted.

The black Lincoln jumped ahead and sped up the road toward the tall security gates. "You heard the man... let's go!" said Tina.

"If you insist, but I'd rather stay here in your arms for a while."

"A romanticist, just as I've always suspected," she giggled girlishly. "There's work to be done and you just wanna watch the bay."

"In your arms, my love. But you're right, we'd better get moving or the gate'll close behind them."

They jumped into the Honda and followed the Jastrow Brothers into the estate, past the armed guards and iron gates. Two men, dressed in brown overcoats and matching cocked brim fedora-type hats, were each heavily armed with what appeared to be automatic rifles.

They passed the guards swiftly, following the Lincoln on a narrow drive through a dense grove of tall douglas firs; long thick needled branches shimmering in poetic unison in the gentle sea breeze. They drove through the tall trees and approached the huge concrete parking area in front of the elegant tural structure that Aron and Patricia Jastrow called home. Brandon parked near the front of the building while Aron, Patricia and Richard got out of their car. A young man, dark complexioned in a white suit, quickly jumped into the Lincoln and drove it around the house, out of sight, into the huge multi-stalled maintenance garage.

Aron Jastrow smiled warmly at Tina and

Brandon from the wide concrete steps which led up to a short walkway to the entryway and front doors of their home. "Welcome to Jastrow. It appears that we're the first to arrive, but I'm sure the rest of our guests'll be along shortly."

"This is nice, Aron," said Brandon. He and Tina strolled arm in arm up the steps, joining the three as they stood on the front porch. "How'd it withstand the seven-pointer on Tuesday?"

"Not a dish broken or a thing out of place."

Brandon stopped for a second, then gazed around at the gardens surrounding the mansion, the unbroken windows and the seemingly undamaged structure. "What happened? Did the quake miss Tiburon?"

"Not really. There was damage in town, and to several of the older buildings out there," he laughed. "You see, I had this building designed and built with the best technology available today in earthquake proofing."

"My husband knows all about it, being involved in commercial real estate. Living in San Francisco, one must take earthquake safety into consideration, don't you think, Mr. Harrison?"

He smiled and nodded, then proceeded with Tina up the steps and joined the Jastrows on the porch. "You're probably right, Mrs. Jastrow."

"Call me Pat. May I call you Brandon, and you Tina?"

"Yes," smiled Tina. "Let's get rid of the formalities. I've got a feeling we'll get a lot more accomplished that way."

Richard Jastrow opened the carved, walnut door and the group stepped into a magnificent, huge living room. Surrounded with wall-size plate glass windows along the southern side for passive solar heat, light and a beautiful view of the San Francisco Bay and Angel Island, the room measured nearly a thousand square feet in size. A massive granite river rock fireplace covered the entire west wall, with a bookcase built into the left end of the rock wall. A thick shag carpet of warm hues of browns covered the huge room.

A wide stair wound up to the second floor; a handsomely-carved wood bannister led up to and along the hallway around the east wall to three rooms. Brandon assumed that the master bedroom and a couple of other guest rooms occupied that area. The soft sound of progressive jazz filtered through the home from hidden speakers.

Around the corner below the staircase, the formal dining room, set for the afternoon's guests, could be seen. A multi-leafed maple table occupied the center of the huge room, surrounded with fourteen highly polished, elegantly crafted matching chairs. The floor, highly polished tongue-and-groove hardwood, remained uncovered and was beautiful to behold.

A huge gold-plated, multi-armed chandelier hung from the center of the room over the table. Its glass, candle-like lights illuminated the room.

Brandon, figured as did Tina, that the furniture of these two rooms alone probably exceeded the price of their home. Facing the fireplace, the earth-toned furniture included a corner sectional sofa which divided the room, a matching love seat and two small matching rockers, all surrounding a large coffee table of walnut, inlaid with six plates of glass. The rest of the room was unfurnished with the exception of two large paintings of winter mountain scenes on the far wall beneath the balcony.

"Look at the size of this room," whispered Tina. "It's huge!"

"Must be fifty by fifty, and probably sixteen feet high," replied an astonished Brandon.

"You're nearly correct in your assessment." Aron smiled at him, then looked around like a proud father at his home. "Designed it all myself, you know."

"Really? It's quite impressive."

"I'll give you two a tour later, after the rest of our guests arrive. Come, look out through the window at my estate."

The two PI's followed him to the huge plate glass windows that towered up sixteen feet above them and covered the entire side of the room. Aron pointed outside with a casual wave of his hand toward the garden of his estate. A huge, sparkling blue swimming pool was the center of attention. Surrounding it was a colorful flower garden of roses and various other flowers around a multi-layered redwood deck with sunken hot tub.

Two glass-topped umbrella-shaded tables and chairs with matching white and yellow chaise lounges faced the pool. "It's heated all year long," said Aron. "I love to swim and hate cold water. The gas heater's supplemented by an extensive solar heating project I've developed. It heats the home and the pool. What do you think, Brandon? Tina?"

Tina replied. "But this is not unexpected from a man of your stature. I suppose you also have tennis courts?"

"Of course... just on the other side of the spa patio. You play tennis?"

"My favorite sport. Brandon and I go out a couple times a week and play."

"She's pretty good, too!"

"Well, maybe I'll introduce you to our tennis courts one of these days."

"Richard, do you live like this, too?"

"No, Miss Wolffe. Mine is less entertainment and a more casual style of life."

"Richard doesn't surround himself with the sweet amenities of life. He prefers his large condo in the city," said Patricia.

"That's right, dear sister. I prefer to live near the action and my office, although I am quite good at tennis."

The door chimes rang out in melodic harmony, alerting the group to the arrival of some of the guests. Patricia gracefully walked across the living room to answer the chimes and welcome her guests.

"My wife loves to entertain. Anytime is a good time for a party." Aron Jastrow smiled, shook his head wearily, and straightened his large overweight body, pulling in his stomach. Gazing into Brandon's eyes, he grinned boyishly. "I must keep up appearances, right? Our guests are arriving."

"Just what is the purpose of this reception, Aron?" asked Tina. "I mean, why are you having all these people from the funeral here today?"

"Why... to help you solve the mystery, of course."

"Of course," retorted Brandon.

"Don't you see? Everyone who knew our dearly departed friends, Dan and Sarah, will be here in one place. Maybe this wake, shall we call it, will reveal the true identity of the murderer."

"I like your motive, Aron." Brandon smiled and put his arm around Tina's slim waist. She glanced into Aron's laughing eyes, then up into Brandon's. Patricia Jastrow's surprised voice carried across the room as she opened the front door. "Katie! Come in! We missed you at the cemetery!"

Chapter Nineteen

"Hello", Pat. Sorry I missed the grave-side services." Katie Denton strolled by Pat Jastrow, her scarlet, short-cropped red hair demanding the attention of everyone. Katie's girlish smile beamed at the sight of the two PI's there to greet her. Glancing around the huge living room, she stepped down the two stairs towards Aron.

Bobby Mason followed behind, through the door. Nervously, he looked around the room, but without the slightest attempt at eye contact with Patricia Jastrow. He hurried past the hostess, following Katie in close step into the living room, where she threw her arms around Aron, a happy smile on her face.

"I was wondering when you'd get here."

"I almost didn't come, Aron." Katie gave a deep apologetic sigh. A misty tear trickled down her cheek as she gazed across the room at Tina and Brandon. "Bobby was trying to help me escape, to go north to maybe Washington."

"That's understandable."

Katie turned and gazed at Bobby Mason, who was standing nearby, a bewildered look on his face. She parted with Aron, then walked with Mason across the room near the windows to Brandon and Tina.

Tina took a couple of tentative steps toward her in anticipation of an apologetic greeting. "So you were going to leave me here to worry about you?"

"I couldn't, Tina. After all you've done, I just couldn't go without telling you... good-bye." Katie embraced her friend, breathing a sigh of relief from the depth of her soul as Tina hugged her tightly. Tears welled up in both women's eyes at the reality of what had nearly transpired. "Oh, Tina, Brandon! I want so much to be somewhere else, out of danger... the other side of the world or..."

"I know."

"Bobby was gonna help me, but when we reached Santa Rosa, I realized that I couldn't run. I was scared we were being followed by every red pickup truck. I knew that if I was to live without fear of this killer finding me someday, we'd have to find him first."

Brandon, silent, listened intently to his client, who was surrounded by Aron, Richard and Bobby. "Hopefully, you won't regret returning. Tina and I'll do our best to guarantee your safety. But you'll have to do what we tell you, okay?"

"Okay, I promise."

The door chimes rang out once again, a melodic announcement to all that more of the guests had arrived. Patricia sauntered to the door from where she had curiously been observing the others in the entry way. "Diane, come in. You never have to ring the doorbell, you know that."

"I know, but..."

"But nothing, Di. Let me take your coat." Diane stepped out of her long black cotton coat, smiled in recognition of the group in the living room, handed her wrap to Pat, and strolled over to her brothers.

"How you doing, Sis?" asked Richard.

"I'll make it."

"Of course you will. You know Brandon Harrison and Tina Wolffe?"

"We met at the funeral. How goes the investigation since last we spoke?"

"Pretty uneventful." He winked playfully at Tina, who grinned in acknowledgment of his gross understatement. "We've got a couple good leads, though."

In an effort to reshape its windblown effect, Diane brushed back her long blonde hair with a light touch of her fingers as she spoke. "I'm sorry, but this wet weather does wonders to my hair."

"It's okay," said Tina. "It affects everyone's like that. You look fine."

"So, you were engaged to Dan Fisher."

"That's right." Her eyes stared into Harrison's as she answered his question emphatically. "We had just become engaged a week ago, to my brothers' dismay. They both disapproved, you know."

"Di, we were just looking out for your interests," said Aron. She frowned, then turned her back to them.

"That's right!" Richard said in sharp agreement. "He wasn't right for you or the family."

"The family? I loved him and that was all that mattered!"

"It didn't matter that he didn't love you? He loved what you represented... money." Aron looked at Diane, a pleading, anguished but arrogant defiance reflected in his eyes and voice. "Dan was using you. The real estate market had already declined enormously, and after three failed commercial escrows, he was starting to panic."

"God damn it, Aron! He loved me! And I loved him!" she snapped. "We were going to Hawaii and Australia, then Europe for our honeymoon. By the time we'd have returned next spring, the recession would've been over."

Aron shrugged his shoulders at Diane and Richard. "Okay now, we didn't come here to fight about Dan's shortcomings. We came to mourn his death... and Sarah's."

"Yeah, poor Sarah." Katie's voice cracked softly, her face wrought with pain over her two friends' deaths. "Why Sarah, though? What did she have to do with Dan?"

"Maybe she was an innocent victim of circumstance," said Brandon. He knew he'd diverted the group's attention when everyone looked at him for a new finding in the case. "I think that the murderer may've been trying to get at you, Aron. Sarah, being your receptionist, let him walk right up to her desk. She wouldn't have to know him at all, but could identify him."

The doorbell chimed out once more, effectively interrupting Harrison's thoughts.

Aron gasped as if someone had punched him in his soft overweight stomach; an icy, tingling chill ran up and down his spine, ending in a lump in his thick throat. Richard stared at him, knowing that he was shaken to the core of his soul. Patricia's voice seemed to echo across the room announcing the newly arrived guests. "Come in, Michael. Hello, Gina, nice of you to come. I really didn't expect you."

"The pleasure's all ours," said Michael Fallone. The couple stepped through into the living room, greeting each of the group with their eyes. "I figured it would be indelicate of me not to come for awhile."

"I made him come." Gina Benado's voice was just loud enough for all to hear, with a touch of bitterness pointed at him. She walked past him toward the group in the living room, her long black gown flowing gracefully over her nicely shaped figure, attracting the willing attention of everyone in the room. Michael took a hold of her hand and strutted proudly at her side to the group.

"Aron, Richard, Diane." He greeted his hosts, shaking hands with each and holding Diane's tenderly in sympathy. "I'm so sorry. It must be so devastating to lose him. Your plans and dreams..."

"Yes." She sniffled.

"If there's anything I can do, just let me know."

"There is. I'll need to have Brandon and Tina, here, go through all of his business dealings and pending sales. There must be a reason for his death."

"Okay, but..."

"I'm officially hiring them to find his killer and protect Katie."

Katie turned in surprise and faced her. "Diane, you don't have to help..."

"Yes I do. You can't afford to pay them much. Anyway, he was my love and I'm gonna find out why he had to die." Diane reached into her small black handbag with her long, red fingernails and pulled out a check, then handed it to Tina. "Here's a check for ten thousand. I'll double it when you find Dan's murderer. If you need any extra expenses paid, just let me know."

"This is very generous," said Brandon, "but you don't have to."

"Yes, I do. I've learned that money, as an incentive, goes a long way; better than promises, anyway. Just find the murderer. If he's Sarah's, I'll double everything. Now, I'll have a martini."

"Of course," said Aron. He motioned to one of the waiters, dressed in a black tuxedo for the occasion, who carried a tray of various drinks. The thin, young Asian man stepped forward and handed her a drink. The door chimes rang out again.

Jackie, Steve and three of their friends entered, greeted Patricia, and taking a drink from the tray of the waiter, joined the group.

Katie's eyes lit up at the sight of her friends. "Jackie! What a surprise!"

"Mr Jastrow invited us."

"I'm so glad you and your friends could come,"

said Aron. "You'll have to introduce us."

"This is Jackie, and her boyfriend Steve." Katie turned to a pretty, petite brunette standing beside the robust blonde woman, and a tall, mustached, well tanned, slender blond man. "And this is Tami, Kathy and Pete. We were all pretty good friends of Dan's."

"As good a friend as he'd allow someone to be," said Steve.

"Not here, Steve." Jackie poked his ribs with her pointed elbow, startling and annoying him.

"Shit," he mumbled. Turning, he walked away to the window, an embarrassed frown on his face. Pete strolled behind, joining Steve, who stopped and gazed outside at the pool. Brandon watched as Pete said something under his breath. Steve looked back at Tina. He caught Brandon's eyes staring at him, smiled, then turned to his friend and muttered a few words.

"Don't pay any attention to him, Brandon." Jackie approached Harrison, smiling with an air of satisfaction. Tami and Kathy joined her, flirting smiles on their faces and inquiring green eyes twinkling with excitement. "He embarrasses easily. I probably shouldn't have said anything."

"He'll get over it. So these are your friends. Tami, is it?"

"Yes," she replied.

"And Kathy."

"So you're a private eye?" Tami's inquiry was both flirtatious and curious. "So you carry a gun? You're certainly strong and handsome."

"Why, thank you, Tami. Yes, I have a gun, but I don't usually carry it unless I expect to have to use it."

Tina joined them, wrapping her arm around his, and smiled a friendly greeting to the three women. "And this is my partner, Tina Wolffe."

"Hi."

"Well, let's get some drinks and mingle," said Jackie. She plucked a drink from a tray, turned and joined Steve.

"Nice meeting you, Brandon. If you need to ask anything about Dan or Sarah, I'm here." Tami smiled flirtatiously and casually sauntered over to Richard with Kathy.

Aron approached the two PI's, drink in hand and still red-faced with concern over Brandon's statement prior to the latest arrivals. "You're going to have to elaborate on your earlier statement. So you think I may have been the target?"

"Just speculation. It was your office. Unless we can prove Sarah Tulley was the real target, which we haven't yet, it would behoove us to keep an open mind. You could be in real danger."

Aron sipped on his scotch and tonic. His eyes scanned the room, landing on each of its occupants momentarily. "Who do you think the murderer is? Anyone in this room?"

"I don't know, but at this point, everyone's a suspect, including both you and Richard, and Diane. As for my prime suspect..." he hesitated, gazed around the room, then turned to Aron. "I have my opinions and hunches."

"Who?"

"Let me work on it. This little affair could and has brought out some interesting tidbits."

"Well, I want this murderer found now," Aron replied hysterically. His voice reverberated through the house and grabbed everyone's attention with an immediacy that stopped all conversation. Aron stared at the guests, whose questioning eyes riveted his in surprise. He smiled, raised his glass to Brandon and Tina, and toasted.

"Here's to solving the murder of Dan and Sarah... and to our illustrious private investigators, in whom I have every confidence that the culprit will be brought justice!"

Suddenly the building rocked under their feet; a mild aftershock swayed the building on its earthquake resistant foundation. It was a subtle reminder of what had happened to their city by the Bay and of what could still literally destroy the entire bay area and their group.

As the building shook, Tina held onto Brandon's arm tightly and watched the chandelier swing threateningly above the dining room table, which was decked out with the meal that was soon to be served.

The earth finally stopped rumbling beneath the estate and a combined sigh of relief filled the huge room. Brandon looked around. "Bobby Mason and Steve aren't here."

"I saw them go outside by the pool," said Tina. Brandon walked over to the window to see the two men talking beside the pool. "I wouldn't want anything to happen to our prime suspect."

Chapter Twenty

The huge chandelier above the long dining room table remained in motion for several long moments, its many faceted glowing gold and crystal globes, which extended down in several ever-broadening levels from the high ceiling, refused to quieten and stabilize after the last aftershock. The group entered the dining room in pairs, eyes inclined to the chiming sounds of the massive but beautiful chandelier.

Aron stepped in the doorway. A noticeable tension pervaded the group, which stood to the sides of the room, away from the table laden with the delicious feast which had been prepared by his kitchen staff.

Brandon said, "That's a pretty ominous structure to sit under, don't you think?"

Aron turned slightly and caught his meaning as their eyes met. "Hmm, I think you're right. Maybe we should eat in the living room. What do you think, Harrison?"

Suddenly the floor moved under their feet again. The immediate reaction was to look up at a now gracefully swinging chandelier, its movement dictating the course of action predominant in each guest's thoughts. "I think you've got a good idea, Aron. Everyone would be a lot more comfortable by the fireplace."

"Okay everyone, let's all move to a safer area... away from the chandelier. We'll have the dinner served in the living room. If you'll all move back, I'll have the tables moved and reset."

The group responded spontaneously by quickly evacuating the room, excitedly talking amongst themselves about the quake. "That had to be a four, at least," said Steve.

Jackie's eyes were still turned up to the ceiling as she walked past Harrison and Tina, standing near the door with Katie and Aron. "I hope that chandelier is bolted into the ceiling real tight, Mr Jastrow."

"Don't worry, Jackie. It'll never come down."

They continued on, followed by Bobby Mason, surrounded by Jackie's two female friends, Tami and Kathy. The two women laughed with giggles and big smiles, their eyes merry with delight, margaritas in hand as they moved gracefully beside Mason. He shrugged his shoulders and smiled at Katie, an apologetic expression on his face. Hesitating momentarily, he was pushed on by his escorts. Pete, towering above them, followed close behind apparently undisturbed by the scene.

Mike Fallone, accompanied by Gina, followed them. "Looks like Bobby's found himself some new toys."

"Mike!" Gina glared at him angrily. "You've no right to say that. Just shut up."

"Sorry. I didn't mean to..."

"It's okay," said Katie. "I understood your meaning. He's always like that, but he cares for me... and loves me, too." Her voice cracked on the verge of jealous tears as she watched her man take a seat on the sofa in front of the fireplace with the two women.

The kitchen staff promptly relocated the food to one side of the living room on lightweight portable tables. It became a buffet-style lunch instead of a sit-down meal, which was fine with Harrison. He would be able to mingle, circulate through the group seeking out answers and clues to the missing pieces of the case. Jackie and Steve, who stood near the bookshelves along the left side of the massive fireplace, were first on his list of people who may supply information on possible motives among the suspect guests.

He and Tina walked slowly, along with Katie, to the fireplace, where many of the people had gathered to be out of the way of the staff and their shifting of the dining areas.

Katie said, "I'm going to join Bobby and Kathy and Tami. Would you sit with us, Tina?"

"Of course."

"I'm gonna have a talk with those two... Jackie and Steve. Save me a seat. I'll be back in a minute or so."

Tina grinned. "Maybe I'll get some information out of Bobby and friends."

"See what you can find out." He approached Steve, who nodded in recognition. Jackie's smile invited him to join the two as Tina and Katie sat down beside Kathy Warner, on Bobby's right.

Jackie said, "Brandon, how big do you think that last one was? Over five or under?"

"I don't know, but I'd venture a guess at four. Am I close?"

"Steve thinks it was at least five. I'm more inclined to be in the same neighborhood as you."

"We'll find out later, I'm sure," said Steve. "Now for more important things, like who dunnit?"

"Yeah, any suspects yet, Mister PI?"

"Tell me what you know about Mike Fallone."

"Mike? Are you kidding?" whispered Steve. "He's not a murderer.

"He seems a bit overly concerned about Katie. He was at her apartment a couple of times, and was detained by the police in the Bay Building yesterday."

"Get your mind off Mike. It's Bobby over there that I'd be inclined to suspect."

"Bobby Mason?" Jackie whispered her astonished retort at her man's statement. "Are you kidding, Steve? Come on, you can do better than that!"

"Yeah? He's always playing around with other women, but doesn't like anyone getting too close to Katie. Dan and Katie were always together, even after hours for supposed business dinners with clients."

"You think he shot Dan?"

"Could've, Jackie."

"What about Sarah?"

"I don't know. Maybe it's like you said, Brandon. Someone's after Aron. Two separate incidents?"

"Maybe. What were you and Bobby doing outside when that quake hit a few minutes ago? I noticed you two were discussing something by the pool."

"He went outside and I just wanted to see what he was up to."

"And?"

"He was lighting up a cigarette. The aftershock hit just as I got outside. The pool sloshed back and forth several times... and I almost lost my footing.

"He grabbed me so wouldn't fall in. When it was over, I thanked him. We chatted about it, then came inside."

"I see. But you still think he's capable of murder."

"I said I'd be inclined to suspect him. As for him being capable of murder... maybe and maybe not. Excuse me, I'm gonna get another drink. Can I get you anything?"

"No thanks." Steve Crowley walked away, leaving Jackie alone with Brandon.

"Don't pay any attention to him. He doesn't have an analytical mind like you," she said.

"What's he do for a living?"

"Steve's an escrow officer. Works in the Bay Building Escrow... on the first floor."

"I see. So that's how you all know each other?"

"Yeah. He works with Mike and the Jastrows on alot of commercial accounts. He'd been working on one with Dan Fisher just recently."

"And what do you do, Jackie?"

"I'm office manager for Luke Iverson's Insurance Services, in Oakland. I used to work with Steve, but I got a better offer with Luke, and I don't have to fight the Bay Bridge traffic everyday. I'm glad I wasn't out on the bridge Tuesday in traffic."

"You live in Oakland, then?"

"Yes. Bobby and Steve live in the same condo complex in North Oakland as I do. Since Bobby's a Giants fan, it was his idea to have the series party at his place that night."

"And Bobby was late getting home to host his own party?"

She nodded and looked around the room to see if anyone was close by listening to them, then whispered confidentially, their backs turned to the room and facing the fireplace, "You don't think Bobby had the nerve to kill Dan and Sarah, do you?"

"I'm not sure. Do you think he could've?"

"No. Definitely not."

"So, you and Steve and a couple others were waiting for him at his apartment until the quake hit, is that right?"

"Me and Tami and Kathy, and a couple others. But Steve hadn't gotten home yet. See, he got caught in the earthquake at work and didn't make it home till the next morning."

"He was at work in the Bay Building?"

"That's right. He said it was crazy. He thought

the whole Bay Building was gonna come down on him."

"Interesting. He can be placed in the Bay Building, near the scene of the crime."

"You don't think Steve had anything to do with it?"

"No, Jackie. But he may know something, or be able to fill in some information on people there."

"If you have any more questions, please don't hesitate to ask. I'm sure he'd be happy to help, too."

"Thanks. I'm gonna check in with Tina. You've been a big help already." He smiled, then joined Tina.

"Brandon," Tina whispered. He sat beside her and Katie. "Apparently, Bobby made it to Oakland before the quake, stopping at a store to pick up a few more things. He saw the Nimitz crash down when the quake hit, and stayed all night to help get victims out."

"That's why he didn't get home till next day," said Katie, in a low whisper.

"All we've heard are heroic stories of how he helped rescue people from their cars during the Nimitz disaster."

"It must have been awful. All those poor people, crushed in their cars..." Katie sighed.

"Can he verify his story?"

"Apparently, he worked closely with search and rescue teams of the police and fire departments."

"We'll have Garth check it out. Meanwhile, shall we go stand in line for some food?"

"Good idea. Come on, Katie."

Katie glanced over at her man surrounded on both sides by Tami and Kathy, a forlorn look on her face. She nodded, then said, "Bobby, can I talk to you alone?"

He smiled with the sudden realization that he'd been virtually ignoring Katie. Standing up, he smiled at his two interested friends, pardoned himself and approached Katie, who now stood in front of the fireplace. "I'm sorry, Katie. I didn't mean to ignore you, I guess I got caught up in my story."

"I understand. Would you escort me to the table for dinner?"

"Sure. After we eat, let's get out of here. We're all packed up. You can come over to my place, then..." He glanced around to see Brandon and Tina walk away toward the table. "We'll get an early start for Washington."

"I've got other plans! I've got to stay here and help Tina and Brandon."

"What? Shit, you could get killed out there!"

"Damn it, Bobby... I have to stay! I can't just run away... I've already tried that, remember? I'm going home with Tina and staying with them until it's all over."

"Great! Just great!" Bobby Mason's face flushed red with anger as he retorted in a harsh whisper, "I'll stay in Oakland. I don't need to be shot at by someone who's out to get you!"

"Oh, come on, Bobby. Stay with me, like last night. I need you."

"Sorry. There are safer places to be in life, and being with you in the city isn't. You come away with me, and I'll stay with you."

Puzzled, she gazed into his frightened eyes. She noticed a bead of perspiration or two roll down Bobby's cheek from his neatly trimmed dark sideburn. Looking across the room to the table at Tina and Brandon, she made up her mind. "I'll think about it. Now, let's go over to get some food."

Brandon watched Steve dab a large spoonful

of fruit salad onto his plate, then repeat with an identical amount on Jackie's plate. "That looks pretty good, huh, Tina?"

"Yes. I'll have a little, too." Steve smiled, as he handed her the spoon. "Everything looks so good. Guess I'll start out with just a little, Brandon."

Steve said, "You're so thin and nicely shaped. I'll bet you don't eat a lot."

"Oh, I eat plenty, as Brandon can attest to. Right, honey?"

"She eats us outta house and home." He laughed and placed two pieces of medium rare roast beef on his plate, then two on Tina's plate. "Speaking of house and home, I hear you live near Bobby and Jackie."

"Same complex."

"And you were going to be at Bobby's World Series party, but he didn't make it home?"

"Just like him, though. We've got enough. Excuse us while we go find a place to eat." Steve stared into Brandon's eyes momentarily, smiled at Tina, then walked away with Jackie.

"My little voice is trying to tell me something."

"Yeah? Like what?"

"Steve. We should find out more about him. He keeps pointing the finger at Bobby for some reason."

"So?"

"So, he works in the Bay Building and has been placed there at the time of the earthquake and the murders. Tina, I think I've got another suspect."

"We've got too many. We're gonna have to start eliminating them, one by one."

"Motive. I need to find the motive. It's mixed in here somewhere. It's like this tossed green salad. There's a radish at the bottom and that's what we've got to find, by stirring it up to the top."

Chapter Twenty-One

The wake continued on into the late afternoon. To the west, dark clouds began to gather beyond the Golden Gate Bridge with the coming of the next northern storm front out on the Pacific. San Francisco, still digging out the few remaining victims from the rubble created by the massive earthquake four days earlier, prepared for the next predicted onslaught of Mother Nature to hit its coastline within a few hours.

Harrison watched the clouds in the west through one of the tall windows in Jastrow's living room and listened in on a conversation between Steve Crowley and Tina Wolffe. He was particularly conscious of Steve's role in the group of suspects, hoping he might impart a vital lead to the investigation. Since Steve worked in the Bay Building and was placed there during the quake and murders, he was worth the effort.

The two talked socially, enjoying conversation from politics to four-wheeling on the beaches. Tina seemed to have caught Steve's undivided attention. The two obviously didn't want anyone to join in, or so it appeared to Harrison. He moved off across the living room toward the tables of food where Bobby Mason, accompanied by Katie, retold his story to Diane Jastrow, Mike Fallone and Gina.

He averted the group consciously, opting for a conversation with Tami, who was eyeing the many desserts on the far end of the table. Intently, the petite brunette selected three large red strawberries from a bowl. One by one, she scrutinized each before placing it on her plate.

"No wonder you're so small, Tami. Desserts

like that'll hardly put much weight on you."

"I have to work at it, Brandon." She smiled. Her green eyes twinkled.

Brandon gazed over her petite body momentarily, smiled apologetically and approached her. "What'd you mean, work at it?"

"Well, it's hard to avoid eating all that scrumptious cake and ice cream and cookies. But... oh well! I have to keep the my beautiful figure, so this is what I choose to eat instead, see? Strawberries, slices of cantaloupe and watermelon."

"Tasty choices."

"What are you having? Anything?"

"Not just yet. Like you, I try to avoid desserts. I've already eaten enough. Maybe later, after I digest some of that dinner."

"You don't look like you worry much about weight. I'd say you weightlift, jog, and maybe... a little swimming too?"

"Right on all counts." Brandon and Tami walked slowly to the fireplace and sat down on the red brick hearth in front of the wood fire that burned warm. She placed her plate on her lap and picked out a strawberry, then put it to her lush red lips and took a small bite of it. "I'll bet you're into aerobics and exercise, too."

"I love aerobics. Kathy and I belong to a women's aerobic center in Berkeley. We go at least four nights a week. We can't get Jackie to go. She likes country and western dancing, which is fun, I guess."

"Tell me, have you known Bob Mason for a while?"

"I live in the same condo complex. So does Kathy. We're all neighbors!"

"Were you going to be at the World Series party at Bobby's?"

"Oh yes... we were there. It was something, right?"

"What's that, Tami?"

"How Bobby helped rescue all those people from the collapsed Nimitz. He's a real hero!" Tami edged away from the fire, balancing the plate on her lap with one hand and lifting her brown shoulder-length hair with the other, cooling her neck. "It's getting hot here, but it feels good. I'm always cold. Feel my hand."

She placed her thin, small hand into Brandon's and smiled. "It's cold! Why'd you move away from the heat?"

"Just to cool my back. You're warm. What's it like to be a PI? I bet it's fun. Lots of excitement and death-defying action, right?" Tami stared into his eyes with intense excitement, holding her breath for his reply.

"It has its moments." The excitement on her face turned into a question almost instantly. "It's mostly just divorce cases and insurance investigations.

Of course, there's always the occasional murder investigation to keep me on my toes."

"Like this one!" She peered around at the guests to make sure no one was listening or standing nearby. "Who do you think did it? Someone in this room, right?"

"Very perceptive, Tami. Got any suspects or ideas on the murders?"

She thought for a few seconds, her eyes darting around the room at each of the guests. Returning her inquisitive but knowing gaze to him, she stared mysteriously into his eyes as if the answer was as plain to her as the strawberry dessert in her dish. "Mike Fallone or Steve," she whispered.

"What makes you say that?"

"Woman's intuition. Mike was always mad at Dan. He has a real bad temper, too. He and Steve have ripped him up one side and down the other on many occasions. They've said some nasty things about him, that's all."

"Well, that's a far cry from murder."

"Steve and Mike love to go four-wheeling out on Mount Tam. They've even gone target shooting out there... which is strictly against the law."

"Together, huh?"

"I've gone out with Jackie and Kathy and them. See, they load their ATV four-wheelers into their pickups and go out to the beaches along Tam. They're going out tomorrow if it doesn't rain."

"Interesting. What kind of pickup does Steve drive?"

"A newer Chevy or Ford, I think."

"Tami! Come over here a minute!" Jackie waved at her from across the room near the windows. She, Kathy and Fallone stood together, watching her and Harrison, effectively interrupting their conversation.

"I'll be back in a minute, okay?"

"Take your time. I'm gonna look for Tina."

"She went outside with Steve a few minutes ago. I saw them when you came over to the table and started talking to me."

"Thanks. See you later." Tami got up and walked to her friends at the window, looking back at Brandon with a wink as she approached them. Brandon strolled slowly toward the sliding glass door.

He caught sight of Tina and Steve sitting at a table near the spa on the other side of the pool. They appeared to be engrossed in conversation. He stood at the glass door for a moment, then approached the group to which Bobby was relating his heroic experiences at the Nimitz collapse. At the same time he kept an eye on Tami in Jackie's group. She looked across the room at him.

Aron Jastrow, along with Richard and Diane, appeared from the kitchen and approached him. "How goes the investigation, Harrison?" Aron's question was posed in a calm, quiet whisper, hardly audible but to Brandon.

"It's been an interesting event here. It's provided me motives and possibly a clue or two."

"Good! How long before you solve the mystery? This evening? Tomorrow?" His voice was demanding, almost accusing.

"No telling yet. I'm going to have to push a few people to get some action going. I just hope it doesn't offend you or your family."

"Don't worry about us. Just find Dan and Sarah's murderer so we can get back to the business of money. That's all I'm interested in." Aron frowned irritatedly at him as Richard and Diane joined them.

"Now, brother," said Richard. "Calm down. We'll just close up for the next week or so until the murderer is caught and the city's back to normal."

"Close up? What are you talking about? We've got a lot of investment property out there to check out. We've got earthquake claims to file with the insurance company. I can't just close down. Just find the murderer by Monday, Harrison. I can't run a company under threat of death."

Diane gazed at Brandon, then turned to Aron. "Don't pay any attention to my dear brother. He's been under a lot of stress. We know you'll do your best and solve the case soon."

"Thanks for your vote of confidence. I really don't know how long it's gonna take, but it shouldn't take much longer. We're close... real close." Brandon walked away toward the door. Steve and Tina approached from the outside as he slid open the door. They stepped inside.

"It's getting kinda cold out there, right Tina?" said Steve.

"It's not bad, but the next storm is blowing in off shore." Tina wrapped her arm around Brandon's and snuggled in close to his body. "Let's go over to the fireplace and warm up, honey."

"Thanks for the nice talk, Tina. I'll see you in a while." Steve winked, turned away and joined Jackie and her friends while the two PI's strolled over to the fireplace.

Their backs to the fire, Brandon said, "Find out anything from him?"

"Possibly. He invited me to go out to Mount Tam with him and some friends. They're gonna ride ATVs on the beach."

"Anything about Dan or Sarah?"

"No. He avoided talking about them. He wanted to talk about more pleasant things, he said."

"Tami mentioned that they were going out there."

"They may go tomorrow, if the storm's blown out."

Tami and Kathy hurried across the room to Bobby Mason and his friends. Both women hugged him and kissed his cheek, then headed for the front door. After stopping to thank Aron and Richard, Tami approached Harrison and Tina.

"Kathy and I are leaving. Remember what I said, okay?"

"You got it, Tami."

"Are you two going to Tam tomorrow?"

"Possibly. You gonna be there?"

"Yeah, unless it's raining or it's too cold. I can

always dress for the cold. I have to work early tomorrow morning, though."

"Maybe I'll see you tomorrow then."

"Okay!" Tami walked away, then motioned to Brandon to join her near the door. He quickly walked over to her. Tina watched as the two met. She pulled Brandon close and touched her lips to his cheek for a long moment. The two parted and Tami walked out the door with her friend. Brandon watched momentarily, then returned to Tina.

"What was that all about?"

"Do I detect a note of jealousy in your voice?"

Tina poked him mischievously in his ribs and giggled as he returned the favor.

"What's going on, Brandon?" she said in a low giggling voice.

"It was just Tami's way of saying good-bye and making sure she'd see me again."

"What'd you mean, see you again?"

He pulled Tina close and touched his lips to hers in a playful kiss. "She asked me to come into Denny's downtown for breakfast tomorrow morning. She's a waitress there. She needs to talk about the case."

"The case?"

"In particular, Steve."

"Steve's not a part of the case, is he?"

"Possibly".

Katie and Bobby strolled arm in arm to the fireplace. A tired forlorn look of apprehension covered their client's face. "Can we go soon,Brandon? Tina? I'm tired."

"You're not going with them? I thought we'd stay at my place," said Bobby.

"Look, Bobby. I'm staying with Tina and Brandon. Come with me. It'll be safe."

"No way. That's it then. It's over between us if

you don't come with me."

"Fine!" Katie turned her angry green eyes to Tina with a pleading frown. "Take me with you."

"Okay, let's go, shall we, Brandon?"

"Yeah, let's try to beat the storm."

"One last time, Katie. Come with me or it's over!"

"It's over, Bobby! Get lost!" Quickly, Katie ran for the front door, said good-bye to her hosts and disappeared outside, followed by Brandon and Tina.

Chapter Twenty-Two

"The storm's starting to blow in hard!" Tina wrapped her arm around Brandon as he opened the door. The sharp wind whipped her long black hair across her face and chilled her legs as they stepped onto the porch. Thick black clouds covered the night sky above as the next Pacific storm buffeted the coast, with strong winds and heavy rains.

"Yeah, and we left the umbrella in the car. He took Tina's hand, Katie following close behind, and the three ran down the wet slippery steps to the parking lot.

The sky seemed to open up, releasing the cloud's water all at once. With the wind blowing at about twenty to thirty miles per hour against the small peninsula opposite Richardson Bay, the rain pelted them like thousands of tiny missiles, exploding across their unprotected faces.

Brandon opened the passenger door. Katie climbed in the back and Tina hurriedly followed, sitting in the front passenger seat. She reached over and unlocked the driver door as Brandon ran around to it. He slid inside, started the car, and gazed at Tina's cold, wet face. She smiled and shivered. "Turn on the heater... on high!"

"You got it!" With that, he started the red Honda Prelude, turned the heater to high, and backed around to exit. The red tail lights of a small car disappeared through the gate ahead of them. "That must be Tami and Kathy."

"I wonder what she thinks Steve has to do with the murders?" said Tina.

"Apparently, he and Mike Fallone are close buddies. They like to four-wheel and go shooting together."

Katie leaned forward between the front seats. "Yeah, they do a lot of things together... you know, the macho stuff."

"They're leaving too!" Tina's comment was directed at the doorway of the mansion, where Jackie led Steve, Pete, Mike and Gina out into the storm. Aron held out two umbrellas from the porch. Steve and Jackie got themselves under one and Gina made sure that she and Mike were under the other. "It looks like the wake's over."

Brandon drove the Honda through the open gates. The guards stood next to the wall, out of the windy rain, and waved them on. The road was narrow, and he remembered that it would continue to be as it wound down back toward Belvedere. The street lights were far apart and had probably been installed through Jastrow's funds.

Slowly, he drove into the dark blowing rain, the headlights of another vehicle leaving the estate followed in the distance.

"What's that?" said Tina. The taillights of a car ahead were flashing red, the vehicle stopped sideways, its front end at the edge of the narrow road, nearly ready to roll down the hill to the cold dark bay below. Brandon slowed the car and hit the bright lights to reveal the small Toyota Corolla and Tami Little slowly stepping out. Kathy was still inside. "It's Tami and Kathy!" Katie's immediate response was one of excited curiosity.

He stopped, turned on the emergency blinkers, and then ran over to the distressed car. "What happened, Tami?"

Tina got out of the car and watched her man momentarily as Tami screamed, "Shit! Its a slide! The road's covered. Look at this! We almost crashed over the side!" Tami's curse was hysterical, a frightened outburst at the realization of what happened. "We almost slid into the bay!"

Tina grabbed a flashlight from the glove compartment and ran through the wind-driven rain to her man. She shined the light inside the small Corolla on Kathy, who grimaced in shock or horror. "Are you okay, Kathy?"

"I... I'm all right. I can't open the door."

The PI moved around the rear of the car and shined the light over the massive mud slide that blocked the narrow road. The car had slid up against the mud, which barred the passenger door effectively from opening.

"You'll have to climb out the driver's side. The door can't be opened because the mud's blocking it."

Brandon walked over to Tina as two vehicles pulled up behind the Honda. "It doesn't look like we're gonna get out this way till tomorrow. That last quake must've caused this slide."

"What'll we do?" Tina scanned the huge pile of mud and debris that blocked the narrow road. "This is probably the only way out, don't you think?"

"Yeah. Guess we'll have to go back to Jastrow's. Maybe he has an alternate way out."

"Hey! What the hell happened?" Mike Fallone yelled as he climbed out of his red Toyota, pickup. Steve and Pete jumped out of Steve's four-wheel drive. Tami ran through the rain, excitedly relating her near disastrous experience.

"Let's help Kathy out," said Brandon.

He and Tina watched the approaching men, their flashlights lighting up the darkness, along with the combined headlights of the three vehicles. Tina helped Kathy out of the car and into the Prelude. "We were lucky we didn't go over the edge," Kathy said as she climbed into the back seat beside Katie. "God damn, that was scary!"

Tina hurried back to Brandon while the two women talked excitedly about the accident. He stood beside Tami's car with Steve, Pete and Mike. Tami had climbed inside Steve's truck to tell Jackie about the accident and to get out of the cold pouring rain.

"All we have to do is move Tami's car out of the way," said Steve. "Then put the truck in four-wheel drive and we're up and over that slide."

"I don't know, Steve. There's no telling how far it extends. It probably dropped off all around that bend. If you lose traction, the truck could slide down the side into the bay." Pete, completely logical in his analysis of the situation, spoke out to his friend. "There's gotta be another street outta here."

"I don't think so," said Brandon. "This is Jastrow's private drive up to his estate. Unless he has another road out the back, I'm afraid we're stuck."

Mike Fallone stepped through the mud to Brandon and Tina, and looked over the side to the bay below. "We can back up Tami's car and turn it around. At least she can drive it back to Jastrow's and not chance leaving it to be buried by another slide."

"You're right, Mike." Brandon climbed into the car. The engine was still running. He shifted the transmission into reverse. "Out of the way, back there. I'm gonna try to get this car out!"

The three men stood back with Tina as he rolled backward and stopped. Turning the front wheels, he shifted into low gear. The front wheels began to spin and the car slid toward the muddy landslide.

"Give me a push, guys!" The three men and Tina all grouped around the back of the car and pushed together as Brandon gave it a little gas. Slowly, the Corolla turned up onto the road and faced the Honda. Brandon drove it up the road past the other vehicles and out of the way.

As he walked back to the group, Tami jumped out of the pickup truck and ran over to him. "You were great! Thanks for getting my little car out of there."

"You're welcome, Tami. Why don't you drive back to the estate? We'll follow as soon as everyone gets turned around."

"Okay. I'll tell Mr. Jastrow what happened. Thanks again!" She climbed into the car and drove away toward the estate. Brandon walked down the road to Tina and the three men, who were still discussing the merits of four-wheeling over the blocked road. The rain whipped harshly across the group's faces, and Tina turned her head down as she wrapped her arms around him for warmth.

"I don't think it's a good idea, Steve. But you guys do what you want. I'm taking Tina and these women back to Jastrow's estate."

"He's got the right idea, Steve. Gina and I are going back."

"Maybe they're right, Steve," said Pete. "I don't like the idea of attempting that feat in the rain. Maybe after the storm blows through later."

Pete and Steve looked out into the dark at the slide as Tina and Brandon climbed into the Prelude. Mike Fallone turned his truck around and headed back to the estate.

"Do you think they'll try it?"

"Try what, Tina?" asked Katie.

"Four-wheeling over the slide."

"Really? They'd have to be crazy to do that!"

"Maybe they don't want to stay around with us."

"What do you mean by that, Brandon?" asked Tina.

The rain slammed into the windshield, driven by the gale force wind that pounded the bay area. "The storm isn't going to ease up soon, and maybe they have something to hide, as Tami suspects."

Katie and Kathy gasped in surprise at the PI's statement, then stared at each other in silence. Brandon backed the car around and followed Fallone's pickup truck back up the road. In the rearview mirror, he saw the two men climb into the truck, and as they approached the gates to Jastrow's, the headlights reflected through the rear window.

"It's going to be an interesting night if we can't leave," said Tina. She opened the glove compartment and lifted her 9 mm Beretta out, then glanced at Brandon. "I'm taking Ginger with me tonight."

"Good idea. I've got Duke at my side."

They drove through the gates past the guards, who waved them through to the parking area in front of the mansion. Quickly, the four climbed out of the car and hurried up the walkway and the steps to the porch. Aron Jastrow stood in the doorway.

"Hurry inside. It looks like you'll all be spending the night at Jastrow!"

Chapter Twenty-Three

"Come in! Warm up by the fireplace. It looks like the others are right behind you." Aron Jastrow's grin, wide and welcome, greeted Brandon and Tina, who rushed up the walkway to the broad steps, up to the porch. They were followed close behind by Katie and Kathy. Aron's huge body nearly blocked the door, but he stepped aside as they reached him.

"Thanks, Aron!" greeted Brandon.

"Is there another road from the estate to Tiburon?"

"No, Tina. I'm afraid that's the only access to my home. If it's as bad as Tami reports, no one leaves here tonight. I've made a call in to my people to get to work on it as soon as possible."

"It'll take hours, in good weather, to clear out that slide," said Brandon.

"Just don't stand here on the porch. Come in and join the others at the fireplace." Aron smiled warm greetings to Katie and Kathy as they entered and followed the two PI's inside. The lights of Steve Crowley's four-wheel drive truck reflected across the parking area and the front door. "Here come the rest of our guests."

Brandon and Tina were soaked, their coats dripping water on the tiled floor beyond the front door as they removed them.

Handing their coats to one of Jastrow's house people, they walked arm in arm to the fireplace, where Bobby sat listening to Tami Little's harrowing story of her mishap with the slide. "And Brandon got my car out with the help of the guys pushing from behind."

"I'm glad you're okay, Tami."

"Oh, here's Brandon and Tina... and Katie and Kathy." She waved excitedly for the four arrivals to join her and Bobby Mason. Bobby stood to greet Katie. Their eyes met, then he turned away and sat on the sofa opposite the hot burning flames in the fireplace. They stood next to Tami, effectively blocking the fire but absorbing the dry heat that radiated from the large stone hearth.

"Bobby?" said Katie, thoughtfully.

"I know. I've been thinking about what I said. I wasn't very nice."

"So, Bob, you decided to stay inside." Brandon smiled and shivered as he spoke. "You're smart... and lucky, I might add."

"Why do you say that?"

"It was smart not to go out in that storm. And you're lucky that Katie still has a forgiving nature."

"I'm not as forgiving as you think. He wants to manipulate me and my life. It's going to take a lot more than an 'I'm sorry' to make amends for the way he said good-bye. It hurt, Bobby."

He looked down, averting his eyes at the bite of her pointed remarks and glaring accusation. Katie, wet and angry at Bob for his indelicate behavior, didn't want to spend the night at Aron Jastrow's estate. Bobby Mason felt embarrassed, just looking for an excuse to get up and hide for a while until his and her emotions could calm down. He looked up at her, a painful, boyish look on his face, and said, "Can I get you something warm, like a cup of coffee?"

Her frown gave way to a weak smile on her freckled, wet face. "Thanks. That would be nice. How about you, Kathy? Brandon? Tina?"

"If it wouldn't be too much of an imposition... with milk," said Brandon.

"I'll take care of everything." Bobby departed as Jackie, Steve and Pete came in from the storm. He greeted them in passing and continued on into the kitchen. Mike Fallone and Gina walked out of the kitchen, each with a hot cup of coffee in hand. Bob Mason barely missed them as they slowly turned the corner into the dining room.

"Watch it!" called Mike.

"Sorry." He brushed past them and disappeared around the corner.

"Hey, Steve! Jackie! I see you decided to rejoin us instead of trying to take on the slide," said Mike, laughing.

"I'd much rather get home, but with Jackie along... I didn't want to scare her." He grinned at her and Pete, who followed them in close behind.

"You'd never had made it, and you know it." Jackie's remark was accusing and pointed, although she made the comment sound like a whimsical joke. Steve knew exactly how she felt, having conversed with her on the subject from the time he'd gotten back into the truck at the slide site, turned around and followed the road back to the estate. Pete had supported his intentions all the way, but still, with someone like Jackie sitting beside him, he'd decided to play it safe.

"Maybe we can try after the rain stops," he jibed. "But in the meantime, let's get warm by the fire. Move over, Tami! I'm freezing!"

"There's lots of room and the fire's hot." Tami squeezed next to Brandon as Jackie found a place between her and Kathy. Aron walked over to the right side of the massive rock fireplace and picked out several small pieces of oak from a small pile, then moved across the hearth and tossed them into the already hot, steadily burning fire.

"That'll keep the flames going," he said.

Richard and Diane Jastrow, followed by Patricia, appeared at the top of the staircase on the second floor balcony that overlooked the living room. Diane smiled as her eyes met Brandon's. She spoke to Richard, then continued down the staircase into the living room and joined the group. "We've got your room assignments for the night. They're being prepared by Aron's staff now," she said.

"There's a lot of us. Is there enough room here to put everyone up?"

"Yes, Mike. It'll be cozy, but there won't be any problem."

"What's Richard doing up there?"

"He and Patti are counting and making sure there's a place for everyone. They'll be down shortly." She gazed up into Brandon's warm eyes momentarily, eager to speak to him instead of Mike. She smiled and looked around at the group momentarily. "This is certainly an unexpected twist of fate... everyone from the office here, I mean," she whispered.

"You mean we have all the suspects gathered for the night..."

"Including the murderer, probably." Her whisper was barely audible to Tina, standing beside Brandon, but everyone within earshot heard. In a heartbeat, the group all turned their eyes on Diane in astonishment. She met them in defiance, her cold blue eyes piercing each member of the group, in search of the guilty soul. Only the crackling blaze of the fire could be heard as the room went silent.

Aron picked up his drink from the large coffee table located in front of the sofa. Facing the group, he gave a stern frown to his sister and lifted his glass. "Diane sure knows how to put a damper on a party."

"I'm realistic about it, brother dear." Her comments were theatrical, boastful, and seemed a bit overplayed to Harrison. "I, for one, am locking my door tonight and sleeping with a gun... if I sleep at all. I suggest that you do the same. Brandon may have been right, you know."

"About what?" Aron grinned at her, then sipped on his scotch and soda with an air of nonchalance.

"About one of Brandon's theories; that you may have been the intended victim instead of Sarah."

"Now, Diane. Let's not jump to conclusions. We may or may not be in danger. But if we are, Harrison and Tina are here to take care of business. Right, Harrison?" He laughed and lifted his glass to the couple in a toast. "May you solve the mystery and apprehend the murderer before he or she strikes again."

Suddenly the lights in the massive home flickered off. The entire house went dark. Tina grabbed Brandon's hand instinctively. The fire in the hearth burned hot and strong, its flames filling the living room with a red-orange glow providing the only source of light to the guests. A gasp rose from the group the moment the lights went out, followed by sighs of relief and murmuring between each other at the warm light of the fire.

"It's okay, everyone," said Aron, confidently. "The storm has knocked out the power, but we do have a back-up generator in the garage. My mechanic is out there right now, so we should have lights in a few minutes."

"I don't like it at all," whispered Tina to Brandon. She felt her nine millimeter gun in its holster within her handbag and looked into the shadows of the fire illuminated living room at the group. They were finding chairs to occupy or were moving toward the remaining food tables, which were still laden with left-overs and desserts. "We should try to leave if we can, later tonight. This could be a hard place to protect Katie."

The two PI's sat on the hearth with Katie beside them. Tami had joined Jackie and Kathy at the table, and Diane stood looking down at Brandon as Tina conversed with him.

"It could be dangerous, all right. But if we play our cards right, we could force the murderer's hand."

"Let's see... do you see Steve anywhere? He was over by the table a moment ago."

Tina quickly looked around the shadow filled room. She found Jackie and Tami at the table, then watched as the two carried their plates of munchies back to the sofa. Tina shook her head. "He's not here."

The front door opened. Aron rushed over to talk to his mechanic, who stood in the opening. Richard made his way down the stairs and joined them, then grabbed his coat from the hall closet and disappeared outside into the stormy night.

"We're having a little trouble with the generator," Aron announced. He approached the group at the fireplace and offered his reassurances. "But don't worry. My brother is pretty handy with such things. And we do have candles and battery operated lights for just such an occasion."

"What happened to the generator, Aron?" asked Diane.

"Well, apparently some cans of paint fell from the shelf above it in the garage. They damaged it somehow. Richard'll have a look and try to fix it."

"Oh, swell! If he's gonna fix it because the mechanic can't, we won't have any power at all tonight." Diane's statement expressed her displeasure at the circumstances.

"That may be the case," said Brandon.

A flashlight lit up the upstairs balcony as Patricia came down the hall and descended the stairs. Reaching the halfway point on the staircase, she announced, "I've got your rooms ready for the night. It's still early, but we'll show everyone their quarters. Then we'll all stay up for some pleasant conversation and a couple of night caps."

Jackie approached Tina and Brandon as the group began to move toward the staircase. She tugged on Brandon's sleeve to stop him and Tina. She said in a whisper, "Have you seen Steve? I can't find him."

"I was wondering about his whereabouts myself," said Brandon. The three looked around the room, their eyes searching the glowing red-orange firelight for him. Katie turned to Brandon and Tina with a look of dismay."

"Where's Bobby?" Katie asked.

"The last I saw of him, he was going to the kitchen to get us some coffee."

"He hasn't returned. Brandon, I'm worried. Maybe I should go to the kitchen and find him."

"No. You go with Tina upstairs. I'll go look for him... and Steve."

Chapter Twenty-Four

The kitchen's damn dark. I wish I had a light.

Brandon moved carefully into the huge kitchen and stopped at the center food preparation island.

Bobby's not in here, unless...

His eyes carefully examined the dark, shadow-covered floor as he continued into the room. A door at the far end of the utility room straight ahead past the main kitchen caught his eye.

Carefully, he stepped inside the large utility room, examined the floor and the shadows around the two sinks, then continued to the open door. Voices outside!

"This is crazy. I don't want to stay here overnight."

"Why not, Pete?" said Bobby Mason.

"Never mind. I just don't like it. We could be stranded here for a couple of days if the rain keeps up like this. And what if there's another quake?"

"Yeah, you'd rather be far away, wouldn't you?"

Brandon stepped quietly into the doorway and looked at the two men. They were leaning against the wall under cover of a long covered porch that protected them from the strong winds and rain. They each held a cigarette in the right hand, close to their mouths. Bobby glanced over as he took a drag and caught a glimpse of Harrison, then nudged Pete's arm.

"Hi, guys! Taking a cigarette break?"

"Yeah. With the power out, that's about all we can do, for now," said Bobby.

"Katie was worried about you."

"Katie? Oh come on now, Brandon. She's really upset with me."

"She's probably paranoid about you," said Pete. He looked down at Harrison with amused green eyes. At six foot four, the well-built man appeared menacing in the shadows of the porch as he inhaled from his cigarette. "What's it to you anyway, Harrison?"

"She's a friend in trouble, that's all." Brandon looked into Bobby's cold, troubled face. "I've been meaning to ask you about this afternoon... who picked you up at the mortuary to get your car?"

Bob Mason coolly took another drag as he looked into Harrison's calculating eyes, then glanced at Pete. "He did, why?"

"Of course, that's why I don't remember seeing you after the funeral or at that gravesite."

"Bobby called me and asked me to give him a lift to get his MG. So I did. What of it?"

"So your MG was close by... closer than your other car at Katie's?" Harrison asked his pointed question.

"Yes. Just a few blocks away at the Bay Building underground parking lot."

"Why'd you try to convince Katie to run away... to Portland, was it? And without telling us first?"

"I was just trying to protect her. She wanted to go to the gravesite first, but I thought it would be too dangerous. I love her, Harrison!"

"Sure you do. Tell me, Pete, how did you get invited to this party? You weren't involved in the funeral at all." Harrison smiled wryly at the tall Pete Shears and stepped back for his response.

Pete stared at him momentarily, took a drag on his small burning butt, then threw it on the porch floor and stepped on it. He looked at him squeamishly, then down at the floor.

Pete slowly walked a couple of paces, then turned to Harrison. "I don't know. I shouldn't even be here. Steve and Jackie stopped by the office on their way over. I was cleaning up a few things when they came. They asked me if I'd like to come along just for the party. I knew everyone there, so I decided to come along. Now I wish I hadn't."

"What kind of car did you use to pick up Bob, here?"

Pete stared into his eyes, a look of mounting anger seemed to surge over his face. "What are you getting at, Harrison? I used my Firebird!" His response was one of frustrated anger. Harrison grinned and continued his line of questioning.

"A Firebird... I see. I just wondered. You have a pickup truck, don't you?"

"Yeah, a Black Chevy four by four, why?"

"Just interested. Did Dan Fisher have a truck and go out with you guys on Tam?"

Bobby looked at Pete as if looking for the appropriate answer, then Harrison.

"No. He wasn't interested in running around with us. His only interest was money... investments, as far as I know."

"As far as I could tell, he was shrewd," said Pete. "He made a lot of enemies. Not many people liked him." Pete lit up another cigarette.

"He didn't impress you much."

"Impress me? Shit! It doesn't surprise me that Dan was hated enough to be murdered. It could've been Diane for that matter."

"Why'd you say that? They were engaged to be married."

"All I know is they had a fight the other day in the lobby... last week on Thursday. She's mean, and that little lady's Midnight Special she carried, a thirty-two caliber, I think... well, I wouldn't want to get her mad at me."

Brandon listened, a look of surprise covering his usually calm face as he analyzed Pete's statement. Somewhat disturbed by this man's revelation, he decided to pursue it further. "You've seen her gun?"

"Only once, up in Jastrow's office. She was showing it to Sarah when I walked in on them with some loan papers for Jastrow. She said she'd purchased it for protection."

"I've never heard about that," said Bobby. "It makes sense, though."

"It doesn't explain why Sarah Tulley was murdered... and what about Katie? She definitely feels it was a man who tried to push her into the elevator shaft," said Brandon.

"Diane's pretty strong. Maybe..." Pete thought carefully about what he was about to say, then decided upon another course. He took another long drag off his cigarette, tossed it down on the concrete floor of the covered porch and crushed it out with his shoe. A grin crossed his face and he stared out across the yard to the surrounding tree-covered stormy hills. "Who do you think murdered them, Harrison?"

"Someone who knew them both. Someone who hated them enough to kill. Someone who didn't want his or her identity to be known, so when Katie witnessed the murder of Dan, she had to be killed, too."

"Well, I'm going inside. It's getting too cold out here for me." Pete turned and walked slowly past Brandon, his eyes riveted in a questioning glare at the PI, who opened the door for him. Pete passed into the dark kitchen and out of sight.

"What do you know about Pete Shears, Bob?"

"Not much. I don't think I wanna know any more than I do. He gives me a chill."

"It's probably just the wind. Come on, let's get some coffee for Katie and Tina. I could use a cup too. It's probably still pretty hot. The power's only been off a little while."

"Okay. So, Brandon, do you think that the killer's among us tonight?" Bobby Mason flicked his cigarette butt out into the rain storm where the wind carried it harmlessly into a waiting puddle of water between the porch and the garage. The look on his face was one of worry. It quickly turned to dismay when Harrison answered.

"Affirmative. It's going to be an interesting evening. I only wish I could get Harry Garth out here. I wonder if the telephones are working. Anyway, let's go inside. Keep your eye on Katie at all times."

"That could be difficult," he mumbled. "She's not exactly happy with me now."

"She's scared Bobby. Someone has been hunting her... trying to take her life. She needs your support, more than anyone else."

Harrison and Bobby Mason rejoined several of the group at the fireplace, carrying a tray of coffee mugs and the large decanter of hot coffee. Katie and Tina sat on the sofa, talking to Kathy, Tami and Jackie, accompanied by Steve. The four friends sat on the rock hearth soaking up the warmth of the blazing logs, apparently happy with their situation, as they giggled and told each other assumably funny jokes.

Aron, Richard, Diane, and Patricia stood nearby, conversing among themselves, almost secretive in appearance, while Michael Fallone and Gina sat on the thick carpeted floor to the right of the hearth. The couple appeared to be content, talking quietly between themselves while Pete, moody and not conversational, stood by himself near the food tables, not eating, just watching.

"Coffee, Tina? Katie?" asked Brandon.

"Thank you, love. How thoughtful. Come over and sit with me." Tina patted the sofa pillow and smiled seductively at her man. "It looks like you've got enough for everyone."

"That's right!" Brandon placed the tray on the coffee table, and by the time he and Bobby had sat down beside the women in their lives, Tami was up and pouring hot liquid like the professional waitress she was.

Aron stepped over to the table as she handed him a cup. He wasn't smiling. "I've got some bad news for everyone. Richard tells me that the generator can't be fixed until tomorrow. That means no lights or heat for the night, unless the power company can fix it."

"We've got plenty of blankets for you, so you won't be cold," added Patricia. "And the beds are comfortable. Just let us know if you need more blankets."

"Another thing," Richard said. "I found out from my men that the road will be impassable, at least till tomorrow morning sometime. So, unfortunately, no one can leave."

"And no one can get in."

"What's that supposed to mean, Harrison?" said Steve.

"Suffice it to say that the storm has us held captive in this elegant mansion. We may as well enjoy the night." Harrison grinned at the group, then sat back on the plush sofa beside Tina. She noticed a twinkle in his eyes, the same twinkle that meant he was onto an idea that on other occasions had led to the solution to the case.

"You onto something, sweetheart?" Harrison whispered into her ear as his lips tenderly touched her cheek.

"Maybe. Follow my lead if we get any reactions from Steve or Mike."

"I'm getting a reaction just feeling your lips on my skin and your breath in my ear," she giggled.

"Me too. But Tina, this is serious."

Katie glanced at the couple innocently, then stood and grasped Bobby's hand. "Come with me to find some munchies at the table, Bobby."

Brandon nodded at Mason, encouraging him to escort her. "She's still obviously attracted to him," he commented to Tina under his breath as Bobby stood and walked Katie away.

"Agreed. And he's not a suspect in my book."

"You're right. His involvement in the rescue efforts at the Nimitz at the time of the murder excludes him from suspicion."

"Who's your suspect, then?"

"Something Tami said earlier about Steve Crowley and Mike Fallone."

"What'd she say?"

"It was obvious to her who her choice would be in this group."

"Those two?" Tina thought about it for a second, and eyed the two men with a casual glance. Her trained mind analyzed his comment as she observed each of the two men. "Mike Fallone's been suspect since I saw him in cuffs at the Bay Building security office. But why Steve?"

"He's been placed at the scene during the quake. Tami told me that he and Mike have both berated Fisher in public, and they disliked him. Mike isn't the grieving partner that he pretends to be."

"Katie should know about any problems that Mike's been having with Dan Fisher. Why hasn't she come forward with this information?"

"I don't know. Guess we'll have to ask her." Harrison stood and reached out for Tina's hand, then pulled her up gently into his arms. She touched her lips to his in a soft kiss. "You take Katie. I'll question Mike."

Tina smiled, her eyes sparkled. "I love the way you say secret things to me. Meet you back here later. We'll compare notes and maybe come up with a murderer."

Chapter Twenty-Five

"Brandon, have a seat with us," said Mike Fallone. Harrison looked at the couple on the warm carpet, legs folded. They sipped on hot coffee together, apparently enjoying each other immensely. He hated to break into the romantic scene, but upon Mike's invitation, Brandon smiled and sat down facing the two.

"Thanks. I'm not interrupting anything, am I?"

"As a matter of fact, we were just talking about Dan and Sarah," said Mike. "Got any suspects yet?"

"I'm working on it. Everyone's a suspect at this point in the investigation, with the exception of a couple of people I've ruled out."

"Am I a suspect?"

"You haven't been ruled out yet."

Fallone, taken aback by the PI's statement, sat in stunned silence as he stared into Brandon's eyes for several moments.

"You don't think my Mikie had anything to do with these murders, do you?" Gina sounded defiant at the possible accusation of her man.

"Possibly. You've had several arguments in the recent past with Dan, am I right?"

"Arguments? I don't know what you're talking about. Sure, we've disagreed on business matters on occasion, but not anything that would warrant me killing him."

"What kind of business matters?"

"Oh, you know... the purchase or sale of a building, the price we should get, which escrow company to use." Mike leaned forward and placed his empty coffee mug on the carpet, a confused and questioning frown on his face. "Could you get me a refill, Gina?"

Gina knew he wanted to talk to Harrison alone, and quietly consented to the task. "Want a refill, Brandon?"

"No thanks." She stood and walked away. Brandon noted that the beautiful petite Gina glanced back at them, then joined Richard and Aron Jastrow. Patricia and Diane walked over to the fireplace, then sat down on the sofa where he and Tina had been.

"Could you say that you and Dan Fisher were on friendly terms Tuesday?"

"Well... not exactly. You see, I walked in on him and Steve during an argument."

"What time was that?"

"About one-thirty. I had entered and heard voices arguing in his office. Katie warned me off and shrugged her shoulders. She said that Steve had barged through past her, madder than hell. Get the picture?"

"What was his beef?"

"Dan went with another escrow company on a deal we'd been working on over in Walnut Creek. An apartment building, about 8 years old, nice location... and a reasonable price. Dan's been avoiding using Bay Building Escrow because they've charged too much and are slower than he likes."

Mike Fallone sighed and looked over at Gina near the food table, talking with Steve and friends. He glanced back at Harrison, who stared into his eyes impatiently. "I like Steve, but he gets mad too easily. Katie told me that the two talked on the phone just before the argument. Steve was furious. Anyway, I went into the office and they immediately dragged me into the argument. I took sides with Steve, even though his rates were higher."

"And you guys are good friends," Brandon pointed

"Maybe that, too. But Dan initiated the arrangements, and escrow had begun. Steve accused him of treachery and deceit. He told Dan he'd pay for it."

"A threat?"

"You might call it that. Steve might be the murderer who put the bullet between Dan's eyes."

"That remains to be seen."

"Well, he doesn't have a small handgun like the one used in the murders. He's got rifles and a .44 magnum. Diane's the only one I know of with a .32. Well, I have to admit, I was pissed at Dan for not consulting with me on the deal. I told him exactly what I thought."

Brandon waited a moment for Mike to continue, then prompted him on. "Which was?"

"Anger and hostility. He had betrayed our partnership to a friend, someone we do business with in good faith. Dan had been doing it a lot. He wanted to break up our business partnership, too. He wanted me to buy him out. Well, I left with Steve. We were both hot! Really pissed off."

"Is that the last time you saw him?"

"Yes. We went out for a drink at Marlow's, down the block. We stayed for about an hour, then I went home, and Steve, back to his office."

"That would've been around three?"

"Yeah, about three. I wasn't watching the time."

Brandon looked back at Tina and Katie near the table with Tami and Jackie. At the same time he saw Gina walking back toward him and noticed that she had a sexy swing to her body and a beautiful smile of perfect teeth to accent her dark hair and pretty face. "Here's your coffee, Mike. Did you have a nice talk?"

"Yes we did, Gina," said Brandon. "I won't take up any more of your time. Thanks for your help, Mike."

"Any time at all. If you have any more questions, please don't hesitate."

Brandon stood up and stretched. The floor was hard, but didn't actually affect him physically, it had just been a long day. "By the way, Mike. Do you know where Diane keeps her gun?"

"Yes. Everyone knows that. In Aron's office, in the bottom drawer of Sarah's desk. She only carried it in parts of town that were dangerous."

"Very interesting." Brandon grinned, and walked away to join Tina. As he crossed the room, Diane and Aron intercepted him. Tina watched while she spoke to her friends, then gracefully excused herself and joined them near the center of the huge room.

"Are the phones still working, Aron?" Brandon asked as they met.

"No. The lines are down out here. You may be able to get through on a car phone. I've got several."

"You may be right. I'll use Tina's in the Prelude."

"Who you calling?" asked Tina.

"Come on out to the car. I need to brainstorm with you on a couple of ideas. We'll be back in a couple of minutes."

"There's an umbrella next to the door."

"Thanks. Oh, Diane. Just one question."

Diane Jastrow gazed into Brandon's eyes, a curious look on her face as she responded. "Okay. Anything, Brandon."

"Can I see your gun?"

"My gun? It's not here. It's in Aron's office, where I usually keep it." Diane hesitated, cautious in her reply. "Why?"

"You mentioned sleeping with a gun, tonight."

"Oh, that. Aron's giving me his .38 Special tonight."

"How many people know about your gun... the thirty-two at the office?"

"Everybody, I guess. I never used it, but when I bought it, everyone made a big deal out of it."

"Thanks. Come on, Tina. Let's go make a call." Brandon and Tina quickly crossed the room. Tina grabbed the umbrella and followed her man out into the wind driven rain. They slid into the Prelude and punched in Harry Garth's home phone number. "I hope the phones aren't out in the city... they're not! It's ringing."

"Why are you calling Harry?"

"Just curious about... Hello, Harry? Brandon here."

"Harrison, what'd you want? I'm off duty." Garth snarled. He seemed incensed by the call, but Harrison knew his old friend was kidding. "Where are you?"

"Tina and I are stuck out at Jastrow's in Tiburon. A slide's blocked the only way in or out. But that's not why I called."

"Good. I couldn't come out to rescue you anyway."

"Why not, Harry?"

"Because I'm tired and wet and just want to turn in." Garth sighed, knowing he probably would be asked to venture out once more into the stormy night on a clue or to look for a piece of evidence.

"Just one question, Harry. Maybe two."

"Make it quick. My favorite TV show's coming on... Friday Fright Night Flicks."

"Did you ever tell anyone where Dan Fisher, and for that matter Sarah Tulley, were shot? You know, anyone at the funeral?"

"No. Not even Jastrow. But then, the Jastrow brothers saw Sarah Tulley's blood-soaked dress."

"No one else knew how Dan Fisher was found?"

"Just Miss Denton. She described him to us when she reported it in the hospital. As far as I know, you and Tina are the only ones outside the department who know the details."

"Harry, one more question. Did you ever reveal the caliber of the bullets taken out of Sarah and Dan?"

"Negative again. Just to you. By the way. The coroner's report shows that Sarah Tulley was shot twice, once in the heart and once in the right chest and lung. It was a thirty-two caliber."

"One more item. Did the lab boys find a thirty-two handgun in Jastrow's office?"

"Nope. No murder weapon yet."

"Did they search Sarah Tulley's desk drawers, in particular the bottom left?"

"Yes. We went over that place with a fine-toothed comb... took everything apart. No weapon was ever found there. Are you onto something?"

"Maybe. I'll let you know later. Did you check on Fallone for other vehicles?"

"Yeah. He's got a six-year old Ford pick up, unlicensed and out of service. Harrison, if he's the one, I wanna be in on the arrest. Call me, got it?"

"Got ya, Harry... unless of course the phones go down. It's a pretty bad storm."

"No excuses, Harrison. Call me." Brandon couldn't get in another word. Harry terminated the conversation and slammed the receiver down, preventing Brandon from making any further comment.

Tina quickly analyzed the conversation. "Diane's gun is the murder weapon?"

"It looks like it. But it's not in the drawer and she doesn't have it."

"If everyone knew where it was kept, then anyone of these people could've murdered both Sarah and Dan Fisher... including Diane."

"Yeah, but I'm really beginning to eliminate everyone but two or three. Diane was in Sacramento when the earthquake struck; that was confirmed by Aron. Bobby was in Oakland at the Nimitz. Aron and Richard were all out of the office for the day, although it could've been one of them."

"So, who's left?"

"Mike Fallone, Dan Fisher's partner, Steve Crowley and Pete Shears from Bay Building Escrow; all buddies with motive, or it could be someone else that we haven't encountered at all."

"It looks like our prime suspect is Steve Crowley," said Tina, in a whisper.

"Maybe... but I just have a hunch about the murderer. We'll need more facts. I need proof before we go accusing anyone."

"Let's go back inside. I'm getting cold."

"Right. I've got a few questions for Fallone and Crowley. I think we may have to push a few buttons on these guys in order to solve the case. I wish Harry was here."

"It could be a long night here on the estate. And it's only nine o'clock now."

They re-entered through the front door and quickly went to the fireplace to warm themselves in front of the hot burning flames. After resuming their seats beside Tami on the rock hearth, Tina noticed Katie wasn't in the room. "Where's Katie, Tami?"

"She just went to the bathroom."

"Oh." Tina thought about it for a quiet moment, then looked at Brandon. "Which bathroom did she use?"

"The one over there off the dining room, next to the kitchen."

"It's pretty dark. I hope she had a light."

"Diane Jastrow escorted her. She has a bright fluorescent camper's light."

"All the same, Brandon... I'm going to check on her. I'll be right back." Tina walked away past the group at the table, into the darkness of the dining room, and disappeared from Brandon's view.

"I hope they get back fast." Tami gazed into his eyes, the fire from the hearth reflected in her green eyes as she spoke. "I don't like to think that anyone's wandering around in the dark with that storm blowing around outside... and Mike Fallone not in sight."

"What? Where is he?" Brandon stood and checked out the occupants of the room. He examined every shadowy corner as he queried Tami in an excited whisper.

"When did he leave?"

"I don't know when he left... or where he went. He just disappeared about the same time that Katie and Diane went to the powder room."

"Damn!" he cursed.

Chapter Twenty-Six

"Aron!" Brandon motioned to his host as he took him aside from Richard, Patricia, Jackie and Steve. The concerned look on the PI's furled brow told Jastrow the conversation would be discreet. They quietly walked away to the windows overlooking the pool outside. "Did you happen to notice where Fallone went?"

"Out this door, I believe. I saw him go outside a minute ago... figured he was going out on the patio for a smoke." The two men walked to the sliding glass door and peered outside into the night. The wind blew through the trees and shrubs that surrounded the huge swimming pool area, but the rain appeared to have stopped its downpour.

"I don't see him. Is there a way out to the front?"

"Through the garage area on the far end of the yard... around the end of the house back there," Aron said. He turned in the direction of the garage, his arms folded as he nodded. "He could regain entry to the house from the kitchen door, too."

"He probably won't stay outside very long, even though the rain's eased up."

A warm smile on Gina's lips greeted the two as she approached, holding a cup of coffee. "Mike went out for a smoke. Do you see him?" She looked through the window, then at Brandon.

"Afraid not, Gina. He must've found a place out of the wind. He'll be back inside soon. It's cold out there."

"It sure is. I'm going over by the fire. It's not very warm inside either."

"Sorry about that," said Aron. "I hope the power's restored soon, but you are right. Let's get closer to the fire. I see Tina and Katie are back."

Brandon turned to see his partner appear out of the darkness of the dining room with Diane and Katie.

Diane's camp light in her right hand was off, but the bright red-orange glow of the fire cast enough light for them to see. The three women were smiling and talking between themselves as they entered the room and headed straight for the fireplace.

Suddenly, the front door opened. Fallone stepped through, then closed it behind him. The wind blew a cold chill through the opening before he slammed it shut. With an innocent look of apology, he walked briskly in, following the women to the fire.

"What're you doing out there, Mike?" asked Katie. "And without a jacket!"

"I just had to go to the truck for something. Sorry about letting the cold inside. It's stopped raining for a while."

The three women met Brandon at the hearth as Gina pulled Mike Fallone into her arms. She gazed into his eyes and held his hand. "You're cold. Let's go over to the fire and warm you up."

"Just a minute. You go save me a place. I need a word with Steve and Pete." With that, he walked away to the group near the food table. Steve and Jackie laughed light-heartedly at one of Richard's quips. Brandon watched from his distant place at the fire as Steve changed his smile to a serious frown at the approach of Fallone, who signaled a desire to talk in confidence away from everyone. Steve and Mike walked toward the windows and looked outside, their backs to everyone else, for a few moments of hushed conversation.

"Harrison, were you able to get your call through?" Aron Jastrow lumbered over to him, drink in hand. It was a martini by the looks of the glass. The question was a conversation starter to most, but he knew that his host was looking for an update on the case. Diane joined him. Together, they faced Brandon and Tina as the others watched and listened. Brandon knew it was time to push a few buttons, and hopefully bring the identity of the murderer to light.

"Yes. Detective Garth was available and I got the answers to several questions concerning the two murders... answers that have narrowed the field of suspects to just a couple." He knew he had attracted the attention of everyone. The group seemed magnetized as they turned, faced him, and slowly moved toward the fireplace in an effort to hear the information he would reveal.

"And just who are your suspects?"

"I don't think Brandon should reveal that at this point in the investigation. It could prove detrimental to the solution of the case."

"Tina's right. However..." Brandon paused, his eyes fell on each of the players for an instant, and an air of suspense filled the quiet, darkened room. From the shadows of the red-orange flame-illuminated room, the guests gathered close together and sat around the two detectives. Fallone stood behind the sofa with Gina as Bobby crowded onto the sofa beside Kathy and Tami. "I think I know what the murder weapon was and that several of you knew exactly where it was kept... in the bottom drawer of Sarah's desk."

Diane gasped in horror, her voice wavered at the implication that pointed the finger of accusation and fault at her. "You mean, my gun? You think they were murdered with my little thirty-two?"

"It's beginning to look that way."

"But, Brandon... I didn't do it. I didn't kill anyone... I couldn't."

"Everyone here is a suspect, Diane. You're not being accused. I'm just revealing what appears to have been the murder weapon." Brandon cast his eyes around the room without the slightest noticeable movement of his head.

He noted the marked indifference on Pete's face, the stunned awe on Steve's, and the innocent gasp of acknowledgment on Mike Fallone's as he looked at Gina. "The gun is missing from its usual place, and both Sarah Tulley and Dan Fisher were shot at close range... by the same caliber gun. Sarah was shot twice."

"This is getting intriguing," said Aron. He walked to Brandon's side next to the hearth, then signaled one of his waiters who was clearing the table across the room. "Max! Bring us all a brandy night cap."

The tall thin Asian man nodded with a smile, stopped what he was doing, and set off for the bar area in the dining room. "Now, Harrison. Do you think the killer was after me?"

"It's possible, but I don't think so. You see, everyone knew you and Richard weren't in the building. No, I think the intended murder victim was Dan Fisher. Sarah discovered the murderer taking the gun from her desk, so it couldn't have been Diane. After all, the gun belonged to her."

"That leaves Mike, Steve... and possibly Pete here, as our main suspects," said Tina. "The rest of these people were nowhere near the building when the quake hit. Where were you and Richard, Aron?"

"My wife and I were at Candlestick, watching the World Series."

"I was alone in my condo, going over financial matters of the corporation." Richard had a sneer in his voice, as if to accuse his brother of negligence in their business affairs.

"My dear brother Richard. When one has box seats at Candlestick, one uses them to the best advantage. We were entertaining possible new real estate investors, Brandon. Potential investors who love baseball."

Richard smirked. "I was alone... no alibi... isn't that what it means, Harrison?"

"That's a fair appraisal. But... you don't really have a motive either. Not like the motive of Mike and Steve."

"What are you talking about!" Steve exclaimed. He pushed past Richard and Diane, leaving Jackie as he confronted Brandon face to face. "Are you accusing me of murder?"

"I haven't accused anyone yet. We're just going over the facts."

"What facts?" Steve said in anger. Harrison wondered what elicited such a reaction. Fallone stared in silence, motionless behind the sofa beside Gina.

"The fact that you were known to be inside the building at the time of the murder. Mike stated that you and Dan had a heated argument in his office, just hours before the murders."

"He did, did he?" Steve glared fiercely at Mike Fallone, then grinned as if in sudden realization. "Shit! You implicated me because that son-of-a-bitch said I was mad at Dan."

"According to Mike, you and Dan Fisher had it out about his choice of escrow companies. He used others, which took away from your commissions.

"I told him to use whoever wanted! Several of

his deals fell through last summer. I told him it wouldn't happen with Bay. We argued about points and fees, yes. But Mike's the guy with the real motive."

All eyes stared at Fallone for his response, who stood behind the sofa, glaring at Steve.

"Tell 'em, Mike. Tell everyone how you hated Dan."

Katie stood and walked toward Mike, her mind reeling back in time to the fateful afternoon. "Mike, you argued more than Pete. Dan told me he was drawing up the papers to buy you out. He had his legal people working on it that day."

"We had disagreements. And he was going to buy me out! Good riddance to the bastard, I say!"

Brandon pulled back Katie. Quickly, he thought out his next pointed question. Fallone and Crowley faced each other. "So, Steve. You and Mike went out for a couple of drinks after your confrontation with Dan. Mike says you were so mad, you could've killed him then and there."

"Shit! I didn't say that! Mike's the one who could've killed him! He wanted me to conspire with him. I refused!" Steve Crowley stomped to the sofa and glared angrily at Fallone as he snarled and lashed out. Grabbing ahold of his black tie, he yanked Fallone by the neck toward him across the back of the sofa. "You're a liar. Tell him! I didn't kill them! Tell them!"

Tami and Kathy jumped off the sofa as Bobby leaned to the side, out of the way.

Steve's strong arms pulled at the flailing Fallone, dragging him over closer to him. Suddenly, Mike swung out in a desperate move with his right fist. It connected with a sharp cracking blow to Steve's jaw. The group scattered as Steve fell backward across the coffee table, scattering the cups and magazines across the floor with the big man.

Brandon jumped up and restrained Steve's fall against the rock hearth. Tina and Katie urgently leapt out of his path. Tina moved away to the end of the sofa to make sure Mike was all right. He stared down at Crowley as he rose, hatred glared from his eyes at the man who had almost choked him to death within the last few astonishing moments. Mike struggled to stand, tripped over Bobby, who was trying to get out of the way, then finally regained his feet.

"You'll pay for this, Crowley! Just like Dan!" Mike pushed his way past Richard and Diane and headed toward the front door.

"Mike! Wait!" Gina cried out hysterically.

"Come on! We're leaving. Slide or no slide!"

"Hold it, Fallone." Tina Wolffe jumped in front of him. "You're not going anywhere. Not until we get a few more answers."

Her menacing Karate stance stopped Fallone instantly. He eyed the PI, smiled and turned back toward the fireplace, past Gina who stood open-mouthed, tears in her eyes at the surprising turn of events.

"You murdered Dan, didn't you!" yelled Steve. He stomped toward Mike, who backed away slowly. Brandon stepped out to stop Crowley as Tina closed on Fallone from the rear.

Suddenly, Fallone's hand reached quickly into his pocket. In a heartbeat he brandished a small black hand-sized semi-automatic gun. At the same instant, he grabbed Tami who had tried to get out of his way. Mike Fallone pushed Kathy back onto the floor and put the gun to Tami's head.

Tina stopped, as did Steve and Brandon. A

wave of fear filled each of the guests in the room. "Everybody back where I can see you, including you, Miss Wolffe! Now!"

Fallone pointed the gun at Tina. She stared at it intensely for a moment, then said, "The murder weapon, I presume?"

"Yes! Now just move back with the others. I killed Dan... and Sarah. She walked in when I got the gun. I knew she'd be the only witness. I told her I needed it for protection on the way to the bank. She refused. She wanted to call Diane first! I agreed, then shot her. When she fell, she cried and screamed. I shot her again."

"You son of a bitch!" yelled Steve. The big man lunged out at Fallone. Instantly, the gun fired in a in a loud violent blast. Steve fell to the floor with a painful cry as he grabbed his wounded right thigh.

Brandon drew Duke and leveled it at Fallone's head. "Drop it, Mike. You can't get away."

"You drop your gun and kick it over here. I mean it! Or Tami dies... Now, Harrison!"

Brandon Harrison stared at him with the steely eyes of determination. He considered the frightened, stiff face of Tami in his arms. He looked down at Steve in agony, curled up, hands pressed hard on his wound. Jackie knelt beside him, tears flowing down her cheeks. He latched the safety on the nine millimeter and tossed it halfway to the gun-wielding man.

"Good move. Now, Tina. Get over there with the others. I'm leaving, and don't try to follow."

Fallone bent down with Tami to pick up Brandon's weapon. Tina moved cautiously around him, within a few feet. All of her concentration focused on Mike and where she could strike him if the opportunity afforded itself.

Suddenly, the earth rumbled beneath them and the house shook violently. Tami screamed. Her fear of the quake outweighed the fear of Fallone's gun. She pushed him frantically backward and leapt toward the front door.

Tina, concentrating on Fallone's head for the last few seconds, instantly jumped out, straight-legged, in a swift Karate move. Her foot struck Fallone above the right ear with a force that nearly snapped his skull and neck. A sharp crackle sounded and the man hit the floor, unconscious. The earth stopped its rumble and a sigh of relief echoed through the dark, silent mansion.

Epilogue

"Brandon, I'm so glad we decided to spend the night here at Jastrow." Tina smiled seductively at her man from under the warm blankets and quilt that covered her on the handsomely carved, king-size bed. "Hurry and get under the covers."

He placed two large split pieces of dried oak on the fire within the huge stone fireplace and poked them a few times. Turning the wood to settle and secure it for a hot continuous fire for the night, he gazed over at Tina. Her alluring dark eyes twinkled and reflected the dancing flames of the fire that lit the large bedroom with an orange-red glow.

"I'll be right there, my love. But first..." He paused and quietly walked across the deep warm shag-carpeted room to the small wet bar. He retrieved a chilled bottle of wine and a pair of fine crystal wine glasses, then held them up for her approval. "A bottle of Sonoma's best white Zinfandel to celebrate this moment?"

"You do have a flare for romance." Tina seductively raised the blankets to invite him inside. He disrobed, then climbed in next to her warm body. She wore only a thin negligee nightie that clung loosely to her petite figure, the feel of which aroused him with excitement as their legs touched.

"Don't I?" He leaned tenderly into her longing arms and kissed her lips softly. She responded, wrapping her arms around him passionately as their bodies entwined, their lips open, tongues probing in lustful desire.

Tina sighed as their lips parted. She gazed into Brandon's smiling eyes. The flickering fire reflected with soft enchantment in her dark Eurasian eyes. "Tell me, how did you put it all together?"

He opened the bottle of Zinfandel and poured two glasses, then handed one to Tina. He placed the bottle on the night stand. "It was something Fallone said... about Fisher being shot between the eyes, and the murder weapon having been a .32. I didn't tell him and the police didn't either."

"So how else would he've known unless he was the murderer!" said Tina. She raised her crystal glass to his, touching them together with a melodic ring. "What about that red Ford pickup? Was he driving it?"

"Yes. Fallone confessed that to Harry and me when we put him and Steve Crowley in the helicopter. What he didn't know was that when he followed her to our house, we were private investigators. He saw her face through the semi-open bathroom window, and shot at her."

"So it was him in the women's bathroom and in the elevator, too."

"That's right. And when he found me snooping around Fisher's office, he had returned to the scene of the crime to see if Dan had left any incriminating evidence around. It was the first time he'd been able to re-enter the building since the quake. I guess I startled him and he shot. The mark of a real amateur."

"He must've ditched that little thirty-two, washed his hands and met the police in the Jastrow office; innocent-looking and with a reason to be there. No one suspected him at the time. I wonder why he tried to kill Katie again in the women's room with all the police around."

"Only he can tell that. Harry's checking out the Ford pickup for the Browning .22 silhouette

Pistol he said he used."

"But I wounded him today at Katie's apartment."

"The medical team found the wound. It was just a scratch on his wrist. It did need stitches, but he had it taped up pretty good. The fall he took when you kicked him must've reopened the wound and dripped blood onto his hand. The med. techs saw it and checked out the wound."

Tina pondered the explanation and took a sip of her wine. "Why did he shoot at me at Katie's?"

"He confessed that he thought you were Katie. He didn't go to the gravesite, pretending that he didn't like cemeteries. He knew Katie had gone with Bobby Mason after the service, and wanted to catch up with her."

Tina sipped on her glass of Zinfandel, her dark questioning eyes reflected the bright dancing flames from within the fireplace. She set her glass down on the highly polished dark wood bedstand and stretched her sheer-covered long legs over her man's bare legs. Curling over him, she laid her head against Brandon's chest. "Katie's going to be all right now. Her psyche will heal, probably a lot faster than Diane Jastrow."

"Diane's devastated. So much hurt and suffering... just like the City by the Bay."

"Diane may never fully recover from her loss," whispered Tina.

"But the city will. The entire bay area will be a much safer place to live as a result of this disaster."

Suddenly, a rumble from deep under the earth shook the mansion and the city. Tina clung tightly to Brandon as the bed swayed back and forth. The minor aftershock, one of hundreds out of Dark Hill, ended in a few seconds, as abruptly as it had begun.

Relieved, Tina reached back and picked up her glass of wine. The two lovers lay back on the large soft pillows, and cuddled close under the blankets. Tina gazed at the blazing fire in the hearth, and feeling the touch of their warm bodies under the blanket, kissed Brandon's hand, tenderly.

"A toast," said Brandon playfully. They raised their glasses. "To San Francisco... the City by the Bay that couldn't be toppled by Loma Prieta...! The Dark Hill!"

About The Author

Born on September 19,1944 and raised in Southern California, I graduated from High School, a musician more than anything else—with virtually no interest in writing.

It wasn't until 1969 when I attended the University of Alaska, after an adventurous summer in Fairbanks, that I became inspired to write. I haven't put these Alaskan adventures on paper yet, but during this turbulent political period of protests and anti-war marches, my life turned to a literary-journalism career.

After the completion of my Bachelor of Arts degree in Psychology, I wrote my Masters of Arts thesis and obtained that degree in 1976, at the Humboldt State University. I became a teacher of young children, founded a child-care centre and preschool which flourished for ten years. During this period in Eureka, California, I tried my hand at writing and illustrating four children's picture books. The children loved them, but the publishers only sent rejects.

At this point, I sat down and wrote my first serious attempt at a novel. I completed my first science fiction work, then wrote two more. I obtained a literary agent who loved the stories, but died before he could sign a publisher.

Then I began writing in the mystery genre and have completed four Harrison/Wolffe novel length manuscripts. With the publishing market apparently closed to new writers, several attempts by agents to sign a publisher were dashed until 1994, when Canadian Literary Agency's, Don Phelan, saw merit in my work, THE DARKHILL MURDERS, and Commonwealth Publications published my story.

Currently, I am living in Southern California, unmarried, and working full time as a commercial insurance underwriter. I am working on the fifth Harrison/Wolffe mystery, looking forward to the day when I can be a full time writer. There are so many stories to tell and I'd like to write them all, for readers everywhere around the world to enjoy.

WATCH FOR THESE NEW COMMONWEALTH BOOKS

	ISBN #	U.S.	Can
❑ **THE ENGAGEMENT,** Woody Needham	1-896329-79-9	$4.99	$6.99
❑ **PAPER CHAIN,** Graham Mole	1-896329-81-0	$4.99	$6.99
❑ **BERMUDA COUNTDOWN,** P.J. Adams	1-896329-83-7	$4.99	$6.99
❑ **THE GREEN DESERT,** Edward Peattie	1-896329-85-3	$4.99	$6.99
❑ **THE CASE OF THE BLUE CHICKEN,** James P. Nelson	1-896329-87-X	$4.99	$6.99
❑ **KISMET,** Tom Pim	1-896329-89-6	$4.99	$6.99
❑ **HELL IN PARADISE,** Kallya Valanis	1-896329-91-8	$4.99	$6.99
❑ **NOT TIME'S FOOLS?,** Stanley Jablonski	1-896329-92-6	$4.99	$6.99
❑ **WHITHER WILLOW?,** Peter J. Ponzo	1-896329-94-2	$4.99	$6.99
❑ **PAN-AM 103,** Alex Ewart	1-896329-96-9	$4.99	$6.99
❑ **BLUE DOG SALOON: A Tale Of Old New Orleans,** Peter Callahan & Tom Bradley	1-55197-014-7	$4.99	$6.99
❑ **THE CATERPILLARIAN CHRONICLES,** Lynne Pembroke	1-896329-98-5	$4.99	$6.99
❑ **WEST OF THE NEOSHO,** George B. Yandell	1-896329-93-4	$4.99	$6.99
❑ **VAMP,** Margaret Holt	1-896329-97-7	$4.99	$6.99
❑ **BRIGHT WINGS BROKEN,** E. Jones	1-896329-95-0	$4.99	$6.99
❑ **YOU'RE NEVER OVER THE HILL,** June E. Weikel	1-55197-000-7	$4.99	$6.99
❑ **SEASON OF THE EEL,** Tory/Rodell	1-55197-175-5	$4.99	$6.99

Available at your local bookstore or use this page to order.

Send to: COMMONWEALTH PUBLICATIONS INC.
9764 - 45th Avenue
Edmonton, Alberta, CANADA T6E 5C5

Please send me the items I have checked above. I am enclosing $__________ (please add $2.50 per book to cover postage and handling). Send check or money order, no cash or C.O.D.'s, please.

Mr./Mrs./Ms.______________________________

Address______________________________

City/State______________________ Zip__________

Please allow four to six weeks for delivery.
Prices and availability subject to change without notice.

San Francisco, 5:04 p.m., October 17th, 1989. The earth shook violently and 274 people lost their lives in the terror. However, of that toll, two succumbed instead to the cold hand of murder. Private investigators Brandon Harrison and Tina Wolffe are hired by Katie Denton, the only witness to the hideous act. Their investigation takes them through a shattered city, and aftershocks rumble below as a vicious, unknown killer stalks their client.

The Dark Hill Murders

by

Robert Ziegler

Available at your local bookstore or use this page to order.

❑ 1-896329-78-0 – THE DARK HILL MURDERS – $4.95 U.S./$6.95 in Canada

Send to: COMMONWEALTH PUBLICATIONS
9764 - 45th Avenue
Edmonton, Alberta, CANADA T6E 5C5

Please send me the items I have checked above. I am enclosing $__________ (please add $2.50 per book to cover postage and handling). Send check or money order, no cash or C.O.D.'s, please.

Mr./Mrs./Ms.____________________

Address____________________

City/State________________ Zip________

Please allow four to six weeks for delivery.
Prices and availability subject to change without notice.